Isabella J Postgate

A Christmas Legend and Other Verses

Isabella J Postgate

A Christmas Legend and Other Verses

ISBN/EAN: 9783337380250

Printed in Europe, USA, Canada, Australia, Japan

Cover: Foto ©Andreas Hilbeck / pixelio.de

More available books at **www.hansebooks.com**

A Christmas Legend:

And other Verses.

BY

ISABELLA J. POSTGATE.

SECOND EDITION.

LONDON:
SIMPKIN, MARSHALL & CO., STATIONERS' HALL
COURT.

BIRMINGHAM AND LEICESTER:
MIDLAND EDUCATIONAL COMPANY.

1889.

PREFACE.

MANY of the Poems in this Book passed through my hands as they were written. I had the privilege of examining them one by one, and of introducing them to other readers. I welcomed the suggestion of a reprint of the verses in which I had been interested. It is an additional pleasure to find in the volume a "Part" which is quite new to me. The work presents great variety, and gives promise of much usefulness.

I do not pretend to be a competent critic. But I am glad, as an ordinary reader, to express my appreciation of the pages that follow. High and good thoughts in verse often find a response in hearts that coldly turn away from subjects presented in less attractive form.

In consenting to the publication of this volume, the author has been influenced by the advice of friends. I believe that her verses will gain many more friends, who will feel but perhaps never express their obligations. One arrangement, however, is entirely her own; I mean, the intention to assist Mission Work in which she has personally laboured for several years.

JAMES S. POLLOCK.

S. ALBAN'S, BIRMINGHAM,
November 7th, 1888.

CONTENTS.

Part I.—CARMINA SACRA.

Part II.—VARIA.

CONTENTS.

PART III.—MISCELLANEOUS POEMS.

CONTENTS.

TO M. B.

(But for whom these pages had been unwritten).

— —

SAINT Dorothea's Roses,
　　Fresh from the sunlit Land—
The white and fragrant Lily
　　That bloomed in Gabriel's hand—

All plants that bless with beauty
　　Or bring from pain release—
Then, by the Crystal River,
　　The Palms that grow in peace—

Such were meet gifts, Beloved,
　　Had I an Angel's might,
For thee, who midst earth's shadows
　　Art "refuge and delight."

Mine are but wayside blossoms,
　　Gathered in dust and heat—
Perchance the love that binds them
　　May make them fair and sweet?

November, 1888.

PART I.

CARMINA SACRA.

A CHRISTMAS LEGEND.

FROM THE GERMAN.

I.

THROUGH the cold streets one Christmas eve,
    In winter bleak and wild,
Wandered, with bare and aching feet,
    A little stranger child.

How brightly through each window pane
    Shine the clear-lighted rooms,
Where stand the sparkling lamp-lit trees,
    Laden with Christmas blooms!

Alas! no comfort can they bring
    This little lonely heart:
Fast fall his tears to see the joy
    In which he hath no part.

" Each child has for his own to-day
  A little tree and light ;
I only have no gift at all,
  Outside in the cold night.

" In my dear home so far away
  One also burned for me :
Brothers and sisters round its gleam
  Shouted and danced for glee.

" Now all the joy is fled away,
  Broken the happy band,
And I, forgotten and alone,
  In this cold foreign land.

" Will no kind mother let me in,
  For sake of charity ;
Is there not, by so many hearths,
  One little nook for me ?

" I ask not, from your laden trees,
  A single gift or toy—
Only a place to sit apart,
  And see the children's joy."

Timid he knocked at gate and door ;
  But deaf were all within :
None came, with gentle voice and hand,
  To bid him welcome in.

The parents gave the Christmas gifts,
    And on their children smiled :
Each thought of his own little ones ;
    None of the lonely child.

" O holy gracious Christ," he cries,
    " No parent have I here ;
No help is left save only Thee,
    O Jesu blest and dear ! "

He rubs his little frost-chilled hand,
    And, stiff with cold and pain,
Lingers to watch the casements' glow,
    Crouched in a narrow lane.

II.

God hears the prayer that man denies—
    For see ! a lovely sight,
A glory clearer than the sun
    Makes the dark alley bright ;

While, gliding soft in snow-white robe,
    There came *another* Child :
Like music from the Heavenly Land
    Sounded his accents mild—

" I am the Blessed Christ," he said,
    "Once born a child like thee :
Poor little lone forsaken one,
    Thou art most dear to Me.

" A tree more lovely far than all
    Which thou hast seen to-night,
I will Myself uprear for thee
    Under the sky's clear height."

Thus graciously the Christ-Child spake,
    And waved to Heaven His Hand,
When lo ! more fair than earth's best blooms
    Behold the Tree doth stand !

How full of clustered stars it gleams,
    With branches wide outspread,
While wondrous radiance, far and near,
    Its Heaven-lit tapers shed !

The child looks up with deep wide eyes ;
    Strange awe his breast doth fill :
Then, gazing on the Heavenly sight,
    The little heart grew still.

It seemed to him a lovely dream ;
    Till, bending from the Tree,
Fair white-winged Angels reach their hands
    And draw him lovingly :

And, from earth's narrow, darksome ways,
    By sin and woe defiled,
The Saviour's gracious Arms once more
    Take up a little child.

He lay, a stiff and lifeless form,
    In morning grey and chill :
And they who found him, wond'ring saw
    The pale lips smiling still.

Thank God ! no more in cold and pain
    The little wanderer sighs ;
And soon forgotten is earth's grief
    In peace of Paradise !

NOEL!

THIS Day may every weight be lifted
    From weary heart and brain,
While once more through earth's clouds, star-rifted,
    Soft floats the Angel strain!

This Day may troops, white-robed and shining,
    Descend the Heavenly stair,
And shower, from gracious hands and loving,
    Such gifts as Angels bear!

May Christ, the King of earth and Heaven,
    The Babe on Mary's breast,
Grant us this Day His Benediction,
    And evermore, His Rest!

III.

CAROL.

How calm lies each hill and green valley
 Hushed into a silence deep,
While earth holds her sleeping children
 As still as her folded sheep!

In wonder and rapt adoration
 All Heaven expectant waits,
Till the bright-winged Herald full gladly
 Shall pass through its shining gates.

To the plains where the flocks are resting,
 Swift speeding at God's command,
He draweth night's dark purple curtain
 Aside with a gentle hand.

Behold, then, how glories of Heaven
 Through the rifted ether pour!
O list to a jubilant chorus
 That echoes for evermore!

For God, in His wonderful mercy,
 Peace and goodwill hath given;
And for us men and our salvation
 The Word hath come from Heaven.

O hasten to Bethlehem's stable
　　Where shineth the heavenly light !
Turn aside with the gladsome shepherds
　　To see this most wondrous sight !

How He lieth at rest in a manger,
　　Cradled with beasts of the field,
The glory and might of His Godhead
　　In lowliest guise concealed ;

Who, leaving His Throne in high Heaven
　　A stranger on earth to roam,
Came down as our Flesh and our Brother
　　To bring the King's banished home.

No sceptre and purple of monarch
　　His state as a King reveal,
Yet here, in the might of God's Presence,
　　Veiled seraphs in worship kneel.

And we, His own ransomed children,
　　In His love have yet dearer part—
Brought nearer to Him than the Angels,
　　Let us give to Him all our heart.

IV.

HOLY INNOCENTS' DAY.

"God hath chosen the weak."—I *Corin.*, i. 27.

BEHOLD the noble martyr army
　　Is by the children led ;
And first, among the flock elected,
　　Christ's tender lambs have bled !

Hear how the feeble lips of infants
　　God's perfect praise may speak ;
Learn how in wondrous power and mercy
　　He doth exalt the meek !

Fierce pangs were theirs and anguish bitter,
　　As fell the flashing sword,
And for His sake unconscious dying
　　They glorified their Lord.

Meek doves for sacrifice made ready,
　　They shed their infant blood ;
Then, safe and pure, God's Hand receives them
　　Drawn from the crimson flood.

So, from earth's dimness and affliction,
    They pass to light and calm ;
Beyond the noise of Rachael's weeping
    To Sion's peaceful psalm !

Fair as the first pale stars of twilight,
    They shed a ray benign,
Young heralds of that host triumphant,.
    Which as the sun shall shine.

Sweet buds torn off and rudely broken,
    Ere their soft leaves unclose—
Shall not they find their place in Heaven
    Near the Heart of the Mystic Rose ?

V.

THE EPIPHANY.

S. Matthew, ii. 11.

THEY come from far a King to seek,
They find a Babe and Maiden meek,
    A low-roofed oxen stall :
Yet rightly richest gifts they bring,
This Babe is of all kings the King,
    The God and Lord of all.

Bright gold one offers now to Him,
Whose glory makes the fine gold dim,
    His kingly state to show ;
And myrrh the bitter hour of strife,
When He, Who giveth all things life,
    In death's dust lieth low.

One offers incense sweet and rare,
The symbol meet of praise and prayer,
    Before the Cradle-Throne ;
For surely God is in this place,
And in the Blessed Infant's Face
    The might of God is shown.

Lord, grant us, as the Kings of old,
By faith the glory to behold
    Which Thy poor Form doth veil ;
Within the stable's narrow bound
To know a spot of holy ground
    And kneel our God to hail :—

That, in dark shades of sinful night,
Since Thou dost call us to Thy light,
    We may no longer roam ;
But, lifting heart and eyes to heaven,
Follow the sign Thy love hath given
    Till the star leads us home !

VI.

"NUNC DIMITTIS."

CLAD in weakest human nature,
 Borne in feeble human arms,
The Christ draws nigh, while through His earthly
  temple
 Echo celestial psalms.

Not in pride and pomp of kingship,
 As Israel's monarchs came ;
Wearing no crown, in silent state He cometh
 His Father's House to claim.

Lowly and poor are those God calls
 To see the wondrous sight,
Where, shedding His first beams of life and healing,
 Dawneth the Light of Light.

Here, with folded wing, Death's Angel
 Waiteth a little space,
For God hath granted to His faithful servant
 To see the Saviour's Face.

" Lord, let Thy servant now depart,
 Let his long travel cease,
Since he hath seen with eyes age-dimmed and weary
 Thy Christ Who bringeth peace."

Now open stand the holy gates,
All may the blessing share ;
Henceforth God's House shall be for every natic
The home of praise and prayer.

Henceforth, with brighter glory filled,
The earthly temples shine,
Where, shrined within the houses He hath hallov
Dwelleth the Word Divine.

The Highest deigns in His " sure love "
To make His glory known,
And His majesty, in earthly substance veiling,
Reigns from His Altar Throne !

Here may sin-stained and laden souls

VII.

A LENTEN HYMN.

"Your God . . . fighteth for you, as He hath promised."—
Joshua, xxiii. 10.

HELP us, O Lord! our soul grows faint and weary;
　　More darkly fall the shades of night:
As in the days of yore, our eyes are holden,
　　We cannot see the light.

Ever around us false lights gleam and vanish,
　　While demon-voices mock and scare:
Grant us Thine aid, ere hope and faith shall fail us,
　　And doubt become despair!

Without Thy Church fierce waves of strife are raging,
　　Within, chill mists of error creep;
While coward hearts repeat the tempter's taunting—
　　"Doth yet your Pilot sleep?"

Peace: let us trust Him; have we not His promise?
　　His word of love so true and deep;
Those whom His Life-Blood once so dearly purchased
　　Shall He not ever keep?

From holy Heaven His blessed Angels watch us
    Singing glad songs of hope and cheer :
They know that God Himself is our Defender,
    And see the victory near.

Then let us stand, true soldiers of our Captain,
    Strong in the love of His dear Name ;
Christ leads us forth, and where His armies follow
    Is glory and not shame !

Still let us, bearing high His Holy Banner,
    Bravely press on to meet our foes ;
And He, Who fights beside us in the battle,
    Shall crown us at its close !

VIII.

THE ANNUNCIATION OF THE BLESSED VIRGIN MARY.

"Exaltavit humiles."

WITHIN the humble chamber
　Where Blessed Mary kneels,
Softly as twilight shadows
　The Heavenly Presence steals.

Unction from Heaven descending,
　Rays of the Light Divine,
Make the poor room God's Temple,
　Mary His Holy Shrine.

Like a pure lily bending
　Swept by the Breath of God,
She waits the wondrous message
　Of grace on her bestowed.

Questioning not, nor doubting,
　Meekly she hears the word ;
And whispers lowly answer—
　" The Handmaid of the Lord ! "

Wings of the Highest fold her,
  Bright Angels near her move ;
While she in awe and wonder
  Ponders the word of love.

Deep in her heart's recesses
  The blessed Hope she keeps ;
Trusting His love unfailing,
  Who slumbers not, nor sleeps

Till, in His time's fulfilment,
  God shall His will disclose ;
And from His chosen Lily
  Shall blossom Sharon's Rose !

IX.

EASTER EVE.

OVER the "holy fields" night's shades fall softly,
    To end a day of pain ;
And hide the deed of darkest shame and horror
    That e'er God's earth did stain.

No more, in sorrow like no other sorrow,
    Forth stretch the nail-pierced Hands ;
The bare Cross—empty of its precious Burden,—
    A silent witness stands.

The bitter cup unto its last dregs emptied,
    The strife and anguish o'er—
The sinless Heart that broke for our salvation
    Throbs in deep pain no more.

For a brief space the Form, so marred and wounded,
    Rests in Its garden grave,
Laid by the reverent hands of loving mourners
    Safe in the rock-hewn cave.

Then to the prisoners bound in Death's sad prison
    The King comes with great grace,
Bearing the torch of life, to be for ever
    A light in that dark place.

Henceforth, the valley of dread unknown horror
    Gleams with a ray Divine :
A radiant pathway, where its gloom is deepest
    The Blessed Footprints shine.

Henceforth, its King—no more a King of Terrors—
    Shall come in Angel guise,
With tender touch to fold the weary fingers
    And close the aching eyes.

And we, in the still shadow of God's Acre,
    In hope may lay to rest,
And calmly yield to God, when He shall need them,
    "Our dearest and our best."

In the safe shelter of His Hand enfolded,
    We know they are in peace :
Yet who may say the sleep they sleep is dreamless,
    That love's sweet care must cease ?

Do *we* forget, spite of all veiling shadows
    That hide them from our sight ;
And can we deem that *they* shall not remember
    Who dwell in Love's clear light ?

Are we not brethren still—in one Communion ?
    Is not one Master ours ?
He Who hath made the Curse for ever stingless
    And wreathed the tomb with flowers.

In faithful words He saith, that when all passeth,
  Love doth for aye endure—
And shall not theirs, drawn nearer to His Presence,
  Grow yet more strong and pure?

And if, sometimes, the dusky veil uplifting
  Shows us they still are near,
Shall we not bless the gracious revelation,
  Not shrink or start with fear?

Rejoicing that for dear ones God hath taken,
  Nor prayer nor love is vain,
Until at length, in glorious Easter brightness.
  He makes us one again!

X.

THE SLEEP OF THE MASTER.

"The Shadow of Death till the Morn."

ALL day the Shepherd sought the sheep,
  Calling them home to rest ;
Now His pierced Head lies pillowed
  Gently on Earth's green breast.

She, at least, loved Him as her Child,
  And did her Maker hail;
For in His hour of anguish
  Her very sun grew pale.

He trod her thorniest pathways,
  His Footprints traced in blood ;
Knowing full well His guerdon—
  Nails and a Cross of wood !

To see God thus, the Holy Ones
  In lowly reverence bow ;
But His own brethren mark not
  The glory round His brow.

He bears long years of toil and pain,
   Paying for them the price ;
And pours at last His Life-Blood
   To crown the sacrifice.

Now for a space the Earth He made
   Holds Him in her embrace ;
While soft white wings of Angels
   Shadow the Holy Place.

Soon will He waken.   Night speeds fast.
   The golden Day is near :
See, in the far East glowing,
   Signs of the Dawn appear !

A ray of Heaven's own brightness
   Pierces Death's ancient prison ;
The Angels fold their pinions
   And whisper, " He is risen."

XI.

S. ALBAN, MARTYR.

June 17th.

" Greater love hath no man than this : that a man lay down
his life for his friends."—*S. John*, xv. 13.

SAINT Alban ! dear and honoured name,
　　'Mid summer joy and light !
We bless God for the noble deed
　　That keeps his memory bright.

His was the greatest human love—
　　A soldier true and brave,
He dared a doom of shame and pain,
　　His friend from death to save.

To him, who spared not for love's sake
　　His own life to lay down,
God added yet more noble fame—
　　A martyr's shining crown.

Scarce made a soldier of the Cross,
　　Its royal way he trod ;
And, faithful to the glorious Sign,
　　Fell in the cause of God.

Ah! then as o'er death's gathering gloom
    The light shone from above,
Through his rapt soul the meaning thrilled
    Of a yet greater Love!

No more an English hillside fair,
    Where flickering sunbeams play,
He sees—but in an Eastern land—
    "A green hill far away;"

Where One, His Father's Well-Beloved,
    A Victim without spot,
Gives up His life in pain for men
    Who knew and loved Him not.

He hears that Voice, most sweet of all,
    Whisper, "Thou, too, shalt be
This day, O servant true and tried,
    In Paradise with Me."

Therefore, with heart that faltereth not,
    He sees the end draw near,
And meets the headsman's lifted sword
    Without a thrill of fear.

We praise Thee, JESU, for the light
    Thy blessed martyr shed;
May we, too, tread the Royal Way,
    And follow where he led!

May we, though in more humble guise,
  Still strive as lights to shine,
And show our smaller flame is fed
  By the same Fire Divine.

Thy warriors, may we still uphold
  Thy Banner manfully,
Till, like Thy valiant soldier-saint,
  We fall asleep in Thee!

XII.

S. JAMES THE APOSTLE.

July 25th.

"Herod . . . killed James the brother of John with the
sword.—*Acts*, xii. 1, 2.

"KILLED with the sword!" say rather, out of darkness
 Translated into light ;
From all earth's sadness, all of sin's pollution,
 Drawn upward to God's sight !

The mystic words find now their full completion :
 The sharp sword doth not spare ;
And in the Master's brimming cup of anguish
 The servant hath a share.

Those vain and passing glories charm no longer
 That once his heart desired ;
He seeks for realms unseen and everlasting,
 With holier ardour fired.

Discerning now in clearer revelation
 The mission of his King,
No more he dreams that transient earthly splendour
 Christ came on earth to bring.

No earthly crown rewards his faithful service,
    No crumbling earthly throne ;
But the bright crown of life and fame undying
    God keepeth for His own.

Once, by the Lake, a humble fisher dwelling,
    In quiet ways he trod,
Till on a day made thus for ever blessed
    He heard the call of God.

Thenceforth he daily learns the holy lesson
    Of Christ's humility—
How still the true disciple's greatest glory
    Is as His Lord to be.

One of the chosen three, in close communion
    Drawn nearer to the Lord ;
He bears the Cross through shame and tribulation,
    Then wins the great reward.

Once more the Voice, whose thrilling sweetness reached
    him,
    Borne on the wind's soft breath,
Bids him arise and witness to his Master,
    Passing to Life through death.

Once more, as leaving all he held most precious,
    He rose without delay,
He follows now in faith and love unfaltering
    The strait and thorny way.

Sharp was the pang, O true and faithful Martyr,
    That loosed thy fleshly chain,
But who may measure what exceeding glory
    Atones for thy brief pain?

Beyond the swift flash of the ruthless weapon
    The glorious guerdon lies,
Amid death's darkness gleam the white-winged Angels
    And whisper, " Paradise ! "

XIII.

S. MICHAEL AND ALL ANGELS.

September 29th.

FOR all the blessed Angels
  Who serve around Thy Feet,
Accept, O Loving JESU,
  A hymn of worship meet!

Michael, the strong Archangel,
  The Warrior of the Lord,
Who, in each hour of peril,
  Unsheathes his mighty sword.

Gabriel, who to the Purest,
  Sent with the lily bloom,
Brightened with beams from Heaven
  Blest Mary's humble room.

And that most gentle Angel,
  Who, when in garden glade
Thy soul grew faint with anguish,
  Came near with Heavenly aid.

For all our Guardian Angels,
   Thy ministers of grace,
But most for those beholding
   In Heaven Thy Father's Face!

That we, though tempted sorely,
   May keep our innocence,
Grant us Thy pure strong Angels
   For succour and defence!

Strengthen our weak endeavours ;
   Help us to faithful stand ;
Take us in Love's due season
   Home to the Angel's Land!

XIV.

ALL SAINTS' DAY.

November 1st.

ABOUT us the dead leaves are falling,
    Nipped off by the chill wind's breath;
All the voices of nature calling
    Speak but of decay and death.

Yet, a light amid darkness springing,
    Comes the Church's song of praise :
Sweet as music from far chimes ringing
    The anthem her children raise ;

As she calls them in glad strains blended
    To honour the pure and blest,
To whom, now their conflict is ended,
    God gives His Eternal Rest.

How calmly on earth's bosom sleeping
    Whom Christ for His own receives,
They wait for the glorious reaping,
    The harvest of golden sheaves !

Gentle plants of our Lord's own sowing
 Made fair with His precious Blood,
'Mid earth's thistles and rank weeds growing.
 How lovely and pure they stood!

Now, transplanted to fairer meadows,
 They bloom under cloudless skies,
Where God giveth, for earthly shadows,
 The sunshine of Paradise!

And to us, who, by earth-storms driven,
 Still wander 'mid clouds and night,
He sets, as in far-off heaven,
 These stars for a beacon light.

May we follow their rays in meekness,
 Until, where all tempest dies,
We, the seed Christ soweth in weakness,
 In glory and power shall rise!

XV.

THE DOOR WAS SHUT.

S. *Matthew*, xxv. 10.

" *THE door was shut.*"   Hath it not long stood open,
    Held by a piercéd Hand,
While yet within the shining hour-glass lingered
    One grain of golden sand?

Did not the Master rise betimes and call us,
    Pleading in accents meek :
" O children, while the torch of life still flameth,
    Spare not My Face to seek!"

Year after year, above earth's strife and turmoil,
    Was not His Voice still heard,
As ever with each note of Advent warning
    The Church's heart was stirred?

Hath He not offered still for strength and healing
    Himself the Living Bread,
When day by day upon each sacred Altar
    The Mystic Feast was spread?

Did *we* not, since the radiant dawning brought us
    Promise of wondrous power,
Stand idle till the dial's solemn finger
    Pointed the day's last hour?

Ah! then, indeed, the hearts of slothful servants
    Despair and anguish filled ;
As the dread cry—" Behold the Bridegroom cometh "—
    The deepening shadows thrilled.

No more, in accents of a loving Shepherd,
    Doth Christ still call in vain :
The Voice we hear is that of most just judgment
    Parting the flock in twain.

Never within the dark and empty lantern
    May wake a wasted flame :
What wedding-robe for thankless guests remaineth
    Save nakedness and shame?

O JESU ! Who art still amongst us standing,
    The Shepherd of the sheep ;
We pray for grace, while yet the door is open,
    Within Thy fold to keep :

Lest we, when the last trumpet's awful summons
    Pierces the far-spent night,
Found at the Wedding Feast, unclothed and speechless,
    Be driven from Thy sight !

XVI.

HYMN TO THE HOLY NAME.

To Jesus—Name most holy—
  Let all yield homage meet!
Veil your bright faces, Angels,
  Kneeling around His Feet!

Men! bow your heads in worship,
  Naming the Blessed Name,
Borne by the Lord of Heaven
  Dwelling in human frame.

Breathe It in awestruck accents,
  With reverent speech and slow :
Sign of the Gift most wondrous
  God gave to men below.

Name! by the white-robed Angel
  Brought to the Mother blest,
Name that she softly whispered
  Soothing her Babe to rest!

Name of His holy Childhood,
  His Manhood's toiling years ;
Name that henceforth hath hallowed
  All human smiles and tears !

Name ! borne with stainless honour,
   When in the deadly strife
He quelled the hosts of evil,
   Winning us crowns of life.

Written in blood-stained letters
   Over the Cross of shame ;
Sign of His hard-won triumph,
   Behold this human Name !

Then, in Ascension glory,
   Raised to the heights unknown,
Where JESUS, the Son of Mary,
   Shareth the Father's Throne.

*　*　*　*　*

We, too, bear names God-given,
   When once in days of old,
Thy Hand, O Faithful Shepherd,
   Drew us within the Fold.

That day, to cleanse and save us,
   Thy loving Spirit came ;
And at the Church's threshold
   Thy sheep were called by name.

Therefore, O mighty Saviour,
   Master and gracious Lord,
Grant to the failing succour,
   Strength to the weak afford ;

That we may give Thee gladly
   All Thy great love doth claim ;
Nor bring by deeds unholy
   Scorn on Thy Holy Name ;

Still, as sheep of our Shepherd,.
   Follow Thy Footsteps here :.
Worship with holy worship,
   Serve Thee with holy fear !

So may we, when life endeth
   And shadows round us fall,
Hearing our name breathed softly,.
   Answer the Master's call ;

Then, with white robes invested,
   Free from all sin and shame,
In the pure light of Thy Presence
   Worship the Holy Name !

XVII.

AN ASPIRATION.

IN hours of gloom and sadness
  Still hast Thou faithful proved,
JESU, of friends most loving,
  Though of all friends least loved !

In sympathy all human,
  In mercy all Divine,
Thou, Who in fleshly temple
  The Godhead didst enshrine !

What if with earthly vision
  We see not now Thy Face,
Nor hear 'mid human voices
  Thy accents full of grace ?

We in Thy Hand are holden,
  We by Thy love are blest ;
And, kneeling round Thine Altar,
  Our souls find fullest rest !

XVIII.

HOLY MOUNTAINS.

"The Holy Mount," . . . "The Place which is called
Calvary," . . . "The Mount called Olivet."

ERE, in the last dread hour of strife,
　　Love's work is made complete,
Christ seeks that mystic holy mountain
　　Where light and shadow meet.

The chosen Three, who, with their Lord,
　　Have climbed the sacred height,
Behold, through veil of Human Vesture,
　　Shine forth the Heavenly Light.

*　　*　　*　　*　　*

See ! Calvary now before Him lies—
　　No earthly friend is near ;
And for the circling light of glory
　　Death with its gloom and fear.

Hidden is now the Father's Face ;
　　While through the darkened sky
Thrills from those Lips, so pure and loving,
　, The prayer of agony.

*　　*　　*　　*　　*

A little while, and Olivet
　　Is very gate of Heaven,
Where, to His servants tried and faithful,
　　Their sacred charge is given.

And how with glory most Divine
　　This " Holy Mountain " shone,
As the cloud of welcoming Angels
　　Bore the Victor to His Throne !

XIX.

THE GOOD PHYSICIAN.

S. Matthew, viii. 14, 15.

ONCE, in His days of earthly toil, the Master
    A saddened home drew near,
Wherein a hovering shadow hushed each footfall
    And stilled each heart with fear.

There, worn with tossing on a bed of suffering,
    One lies with gasping breath ;
While o'er her features, wan and fever-wasted,
    Darkens the shade of Death.

Amid the throng of those who weep around her
    Behold the Saviour stand !
Above the sick in tender pity bending,
    He takes the fevered hand.

No longer wildly leap the frenzied pulses :
    With new-born life they thrill ;
And, owning straight the power of Death's Destroyer,
    She rose to do His Will.

We too, O Lord, wait for Thy touch of healing
  In weariness and heat ;
For still with every pain sin's curse hath given
  Our hearts in anguish beat ;

Till Thou shalt bid, in accents calm and gentle,
  Our throbbing pulses cease ;
And from the tossing of life's " fitful fever "
  Call us unto Thy Peace.

In that new life Thy love for us makes ready
  No flaw or stain shall be ;
And we, with hands and feet no longer feeble,
  Shall minister to Thee.

Then, where no sin may ever let or hinder,
  Shall Thy blest Will be done ;
And we shall know the perfect bliss of service
  When " will and power are one."

XX.

"BENEDICITE."

"God   .   left not Himself without witness.—*Acts*, xiv. 17.

O PRAISE and magnify our God
    For all the gifts of love
He poureth down unceasingly
    From His high throne above.

He made all creatures good at first ;
    And now, though stained with ill,
They keep the impress of His Hand
    And bear Him witness still.

Still doth His sun give life and light,
    Still fall His quickening showers ;
Nor yet earth wearies to put on
    Her green robe starred with flowers.

Nor, in each season's ordered time,
    Doth she her fruit refuse ;
While still the "faithful witness" glows
    In seven perfect hues.

The orb He gave to rule the night
    Doth light our darkness still,
And from the sun's o'erflowing beams
    Her crescent lamp doth fill.

Fulfilling still their Maker's word,
    The storm-winds fiercely blow ;
Or, in the forest, cool and dim,
    Soft breezes whisper low.

The clouds like gorgeous banners still
    Stream in the eastern sky ;
Or seem to bring, when daylight fades,
    Celestial glory nigh.

Still in their silent grandeur stand
    The everlasting hills ;
And still for beauty and delight
    Gush forth the freshening rills.

The depth of ocean breaketh not
    Its firm eternal bars ;
And still in the blue height of heaven
    Clear burn the steadfast stars.

Thus ever in the world He made
    The Hand of God is seen ;
In dreary hours of winter gloom
    Or summer days serene.

Then let His children praise Him still
    And yield Him honour due ;
Waiting in thankful hope and love
    Till He makes all things new.

XXI.

SOLDIERS OF THE CROSS.

*"*Christ's faithful soldiers and servants.*"--Baptismal Service.*

IN days long past a great and glorious army
 Went forth, with might and fame,
To guard the Holy Tomb of Christ our Saviour
 From foul despite and shame.

That these old knights were true and gallant soldiers
 Their noble stories tell ;
For God and Holy Cross their strong swords wielding
 They did their duty well.

And in the rear of this great army followed
 A young and feeble band,*
Who left in faith their homes and loving kindred,
 Their own dear native land,

---

* "In France, A.D. 1212, 30,000 children encamped around
Vendôme ; 10,000 were lost or had strayed away before they reached
Marseilles . . . at length, two merchants offered 'for the cause
of God and without charge' to convey them in ships to Palestine, and
the 5,000 children who sailed from the harbour chanting the 'Veni
Creator Spiritus' found themselves at the end of their voyage in the
slave markets of Alexandria and Algiers. 20,000 German girls and
boys set out in the same year from Cologne, under the peasant lad
Nicholas, of whom 5,000 only reached Genoa ; of the rest, some had
returned home, some marched to Brindisi and, setting sail for Palestine,
were never heard of more."—*The Crusades :* SIR G. W. COX.

Changing the joy and love of peaceful homesteads
　　For battle's din and strife ;
They dare for God hard toil and direst peril
　　And give for Him their life.

Some by the hands of treacherous foes were taken ;
　　Some lost in ways unknown ;
Never again to their fair land returning—
　　Yet God doth keep His own.

Now, though no longer in such earthly warfare
　　God's vassals fight for Him ;
We may not say the Church's children falter,
　　Or that her light burns dim.

We all are called to be Christ's faithful soldiers ;
　　Sworn in our infancy
To hold aloft the Sign in which He conquers,
　　And in His ranks to die.

And see ! where round His Holy Altar kneeling,
　　A band of children throng ;
Receiving from God's free and gracious Spirit
　　Gifts that make pure and strong.

Surely no souls the Blessed Lord hath ransomed
　　Are to His Heart more dear ;
And surely while the mystic words are spoken
　　Hover His Angels near !

Bright may His warriors keep the heavenly armour
    Their Captain gives this day ;
And in the perfect freedom of His service
    Abide and live alway !

Still may God grant for sure defence and succour
    His Angel's sheltering wing ;
Till in the sunlit City where He dwelleth,
    His servants serve their King :

And, after manful fight beneath His banner,
    Lay their tried weapons down ;
And from His Hands, whose love and might upheld
    them,
    Receive the palm and crown !

XXII.

HIDDEN MELODIES.

(SUGGESTED).

The air was filled with music
  Of joy and holy mirth
When the exultant Angels
  Welcomed a God to earth.

The ground once cursed is blessed
  By treading of His Feet,
And still may earthly pathways
  The holy sounds repeat.

His sweet and gracious accents
  Made hearts of men to thrill :
E'en now, through earth's harsh noises,
  We hear their echo still.

Could we but rightly listen,
  Such strains might reach our ears
As in the light's first dawning
  Held mute the listening spheres.

D

One day the Great Musician
　　Shall tune each jarring chord ;
And every hidden harmony
　　Be at His touch restored.

Then far away for ever
　　All discord shall be driven,
And earth once more with gladness
　　Shall hail the choirs of Heaven.

XXIII.

THE FAR-OFF LAND.

"'Thine eyes shall see the King in His beauty : they shall behold
the Land that is very far-off."—*Isaiah*, xxxiii. 17.

A LAND *far-off*. How like a wailing minor
    Woven in harmony
This note amidst the Prophet's song of triumph
    Lingers regretfully !

Ah ! not in truth " far-off," the Land we sigh for
    Full close to us it lies ;
A little space beyond this vale of shadows
    Its golden turrets rise.

A fair wide City, where no rough crowds jostle,
    Where none forsaken roam ;
But where, for all His feeble toiling children,
    Our Father finds a home.

" Threshold of Peace !" How doth our storm-tossed
        spirit
    Desire thy port to gain,
How still our ears, sore wearied with earth's discord,
    Long for thy restful strain !

Yet joy is ours.   God's love is ever round us,
    God's Angels with us still :
And have we not like them a blessed mission
    To do our Father's will?

E'en now, in beauty, thought and speech surpassing,
    The King doth near us stand,
Bidding us follow where in God's clear sunlight
    Fair shines the " far-stretched " Land.

XXIV.

NO MORE SEA.

(SUGGESTED).

" I saw a new Heaven and a new Earth . . . and there
was no more sea."—*Revelation*, xxi. 1.

AH! can it be that earth must miss
 Her beauteous rock-hewn caves ;
That never in God's new-made world
 Shall floods lift up their waves ?

No : but that *there* shall never rise
 Fierce storms and conflicts sore ;
And the " Dead Sea " of curse and pain
 Alone shall be no more.

Perchance in this fair future land
 The waters calmly sleep ;
And God doth not in *tempest* show
 His wonders in the deep.

It may be that the perfect Heaven
 He keeps for His beloved ;
Is earth with all its beauty left
 And all its stain removed.

XXV.

IN MEMORIAM.

ALEXANDER HERIOT MACHONOCHIE:

Born August 11th, 1825 ;

Found dead in Kinloch Forest, December 17th, 1887.

LONG years he bore the Cross in faithful service ;
    Then rose to take the Crown
In a lone place, where watch the steadfast mountains,
    And the still stars look down.

They found him lying 'midst the forest shadows
    In deep and sweet repose ;
Above him—a fair shroud of God's own weaving—
    Drifted the silent snows.

Seeking, from the great city's din and turmoil,
    For a brief space to rest ;
A better rest to this His long-tried servant
    God gave, Who knoweth best.

Like a true soldier, far from friends and kindred,
    God willed to call him home :
Alone—as Moses once on Pisgah's summit,
    He heard the voice say, "Come."

Meet was it, one who fought for Christ so bravely,
　　A soldier's death should die ;
Fight his last fight with only God to aid him,
　　And win the victory.

What if no human footfall broke the stillness,
　　Nor voice of human cheer ;
Call not his deathbed lonely or forsaken,
　　For surely God was near !

Perchance, as the dark shadows fell around him,
　　Fair sights and sounds were given ;
And angel-visions made his stony pillow
　　A very gate of Heaven.

Perchance, soft echoing through the stormwind's wail-
　　　　ing,
　　He heard the Heavenly psalm ;
Till He Who stilled Gennesaret's troubled waters
　　Made this storm, too, a calm.

Not ours to grudge, when from life's weary toiling
　　Our God His own doth claim :
So, for this pure soul, freed from fleshly burthen,
　　We bless His Holy Name.

And for that flock, whose faithful shepherd leaves them
　　Ne'er to return again ;
May Christ, who wept amongst the human mourners,
　　Bring solace to their pain.

May they still hear his voice they loved so dearly
    Speaking as from the dead ;
Still may they keep the words of truth he taught them
    And follow where he led !

God grant them grace, like him, through toil and
    sorrow,
    Firm in the Faith to stand ;
Till they, too, anchor in the wished-for Haven,
    And reach the Blessed Land !

Till where God's Presence gives eternal sunlight,
    Where storms no more may beat :
In God's fair pasture-lands—by His still waters—
    The sheep and shepherd meet !

Christmas Day, 1887.

XXVI.

THE PASSING OF HILDA.

November 17th, A.D. 680.

WITH sounds of sobbing in its waves
    The cold sea shoreward creeps :
Around the Abbey's stately towers
    The solemn night-wind sweeps.
Within, in a dark lowly cell,
    A precious life-flame dies ;
For there, with wasting fever spent,
    The holy Hilda lies.

Behold, in distant convent walls
    One waketh out of sleep,
Hearing a strange and solemn sound
    Startle night's stillness deep !
She riseth straight from pallet low
    With visage changed and pale,
As one who in a vision blest
    Sees Angels bear the Grail.

" Say, Sisters sweet," she whispereth low,.
   " What may such sign foretell
If one perchance in dreams should hear
   The solemn passing-bell?
And in a rapture strange and sweet
   Should see with mortal eye
White Angels with a ransomed soul
   Soar upward to the sky?"

Then forth upon the midnight air
   The chapel bell doth toll,
Asking, with deep and thrilling tone,
   Prayers for a parting soul.
And in the dim and silent aisles
   The pious Sisters kneel
Till, a pale streak through chancel-pane,
   The winter dawn shall steal.

Then with swift feet and boding hearts
   They seek the distant fane—
But no more on her narrow bed
   Doth Hilda lie in pain.
The Heavenly Sign had spoken true,
   For in the silent night
Angels had borne blest Hilda's soul
   Into the Land of Light.

XXVII.

THE CALL OF CAEDMON.

A.D. 670.

As once a sweet-voiced minstrel,
  In Israel's ancient days,
Was taken from the sheepfolds
  The Name of God to praise ;
So, too, the lowly Caedmon,
  After long silent years,
Within his straw-thatched stable
  A wondrous message hears.

To him, poor, lone and aged,
  Amid night's darkness came
The Voice that in his spirit
  Woke the God-kindled flame—
" Take up the harp and say not
  Thy hand or voice is weak ;
For he may not stand silent
  Whom God hath called to speak."

Straightway, with touch of magic,
　　He sweeps the mighty string
To strains such as in rapture
　　The Morning Stars might sing.
In festal hall no longer
　　The harp doth pass him by,
Who sings with passing sweetness
　　The praise of God most high.

Still stands the " wind-swept headland "
　　That heard his melody :
Still at its foot for ever
　　Breaks the unresting sea ;
And still, first of all singers
　　That win our England fame
Shall stand to God's great glory
　　A peasant's humble name !

XXVIII.

THE MOTHER'S DREAM.

(A TRUE STORY),

WHILE on her bed in grievous pain
    The stricken Mother lay,
God took, it seemed with cruel hand,
    Her new-born Babe away.

In patient meekness till that day
    She suffered and was still ;
But now in bitterness of soul
    She murmured at His will.

" It was the only joy I had,"
    She whispered as she wept,
Till by her pain and sorrow spent
    A little while she slept.

Then in a happy dream she stood
    In pleasant garden bowers,
Where One, more fair than sons of men,.
    Seemed Guardian of the flowers.

She saw Him pass those blossoms by
    That in full beauty shone,
And gather, with a piercéd Hand,
    A rosebud scarcely blown.

"How strange to choose a folded bud,"
    The Mother wondering said,
"When glowing fair on every side
    More perfect flowers are spread!"

He smiled and spake: "This infant flower
    Shall blow in fields more blest:"
Then the closed petals gently raised
    And laid upon His Breast.

The Mother's heart, with grief so rent,
    Now thrills with rapture deep;
From such a sweet and blessed dream
    She waketh not to weep.

For a brief space His praise to speak
    God wills her to remain:
Then, as He giveth His beloved,
    He gave her sleep again.

And in the quiet waiting place
    Beneath the Church's shade,
The Mother and the tender Babe
    In one low grave are laid.

Thus did our Father teach His child
    To trust His loving care;
And now both bud and blossom wave
    In His own Garden fair.

XXIX.

A BENEDICTION.

God's love be ever with thee, Sweet,
  Thy soul to keep and shield,
In every hour of peril
  A sword of strength to wield !

All gracious gifts of God the Son
  Be thine to bless and cheer,
As the beloved Disciple
  Mayst thou His Heart be near !

O'er thee, with all the light and grace
  Such Holy Presence brings,
Still rest for peace and shelter
  The Dove's o'er-shadowing wings !

Beside thee still in joy or gloom
  May God's dear Angels stand,
Till, at the shining Gateway,
  Christ takes thee by the hand !

Christmas Eve, 1886.

PART II

V A R I A .

I.

PERDITA.

" I would I had some flowers o' the spring."—
A Winter's Tale.

O GIVE us of thy flowers, Sweet Maid,
　　Or tell us where they grow ;
For not in our most cherished beds
　　Blossoms so fair may show !

Our daffodils are not so bright
　　As those that kissed thy feet ;
Nor can we by our woodpaths find
　　Violets so " dim and sweet."

The sunny south lands now so long
　　Our swallows from us keep ;
Nor can our spring blooms' beauty lay
　　The winds of March to sleep.

Our Shakspere's lute was full as sweet
　　As Orpheus' magic lay,
Is it that when his music ceased
　　Some sunshine went away ?

We search in vain for Shakspere's flowers
　　Our fields and woodland shades,
Perchance such blossoms only grew
　　In his enchanted glades !

II.

CORDELIA.

"I might have saved her; now she's gone for ever."—*Lear.*

I.

A FACE of twilight tenderness,
  Eyes true and clear as morn;
Lips that with pain might quiver,
  But never curve in scorn.

A blossom among poisonous weeds,
  Sweet, fair and undefiled,
A queen in gracious beauty,
  In guileless truth a child.

II.

Such was she once.—Ere yet the dread Wheel's circling
  Had drawn her in its power:
Full in its pathway now she lieth,
  Crushed like a trampled flower.

"Thy truth then be thy dower."—Such was the sentence.
  Now reads its meaning plain,
Her white throat in fulfilment beareth
  That deep and purple stain.

The feather stirs not. Take away that mirror,
  It shows no mist of breath.
No coronet the pure brow graceth
  Save that still crown of Death.

" Cordelia, Cordelia !—Stay a little."
  Is this his voice whose tone
· Withheld once in blind wrath and frenzy
  Grace, love and benison ?

Hers was such love as counts it joy and honour
  To pay love's bitterest price ;
And the high gods themselves throw incense
  Upon such sacrifice.

And what of him who once in fatal blindness
  Thrust from him such a love ?
Is there for him henceforth no solace
  In earth or Heaven above ?

With him, indeed, the Wheel hath come full circle ;
  All hope and help is vain :
The rack now holds him, crushed and bleeding,
  Bound fast with his own chain.

The low soft voice keeps now eternal silence,
  His cries pierce not her ears ;
And " very bootless " now his anguish,
  Remorse and bitter tears.

Peace ! Let him pass. The Wheel hath stopped its
          turning.
  The throbbing pulses cease.
See ! o'er him bends the quiet Angel
  And gives the kiss of peace.

III.

DESDEMONA.

"Unfaith in aught is want of faith in all.
It is the little rift within the lute
That by and bye will make the music mute."—
TENNYSON.

AH! how by ruthless hand the lute lies shattered,
For ever mute the strains once passing sweet:
No frenzied cry its subtle tones may waken,
  Bidding a still heart beat.

Ay, 'tis indeed "too late." No touch of magic
Can e'er give back to the plucked rose its bloom:
Never may any fire of "heat Promethean"
  The torch of life "relume."

Well might'st thou pause, most blind and erring spirit,
And view, with throbbing pulse and bated breath,
The love-sweet eyes unclose e'en while their beauty
  Grew dark with pain and death.

The lids are close shut now; no day shall wake them:
With bruiséd petals the dead flower doth lie,
While the still voice of Death's relentless silence
  "Bids thee despair and die."

Time was, when in the bliss of love's fruition,
No shadow stained a sky serenely clear ;
And none who saw the brightness of the dawning
      Dreamed of a tempest near.

A whisper came of foul and hateful meaning
Mingling with love's clear strains a jarring tone ;
And thou didst listen to the words of evil,
      " Turning within to stone."

Thenceforth, no more the stars like angel faces
From their blue heaven look down to bless and heal ;
But in their very courses seem to battle
      With glittering points of steel.

To nights, by "sweet sleep medicined" no longer,
Peace cometh not with cheerful light of morn,
And e'en earth's blossoms in their gentle beauty
      Seem but to smile in scorn.

Alas ! a " little rift " hath stilled the music ;
A little cloud hath turned fair day to night ;
For Love's clear harmony is discord given,
      Hell's blackness for God's light.

Ah me ! that life with pain and mystery mingled
Full oft a skein of ravelled threads appears,
With no solution of its knots and tangles
      Save the " Blind Fury's " shears !

IV.

THE GRAVE OF OPHELIA.

"I would give you some violets ; but they withered all."—
Hamlet.

I.

WHENCE come these "sweet dim" violets of the
    woods,
Shedding pale lustre in the Place of Death,
And spreading through its dank and sombre shades
The subtle scent of Cytherea's breath ?

This is a place of rest for one whose life
Wrecked ruthlessly fair hopes which once it gave :
These tender blooms, the flowers of love and youth,
Now for all comfort blossom on her grave.

The raindrops on their petals softly fall,
Close to their leaves the sweet wild swallows skim,
The sunrays touch them lightly, and the winds
Sigh o'er this grave that missed the funeral hymn.

How dear to nature seemed this "Rose of May!"
A flower for sunshine and for fragrance made,
Till the storm broke. Then bruised and drenched
    with rain
The pallid blossom in the dust was laid.

II.

Now life is passed with all its strife and turmoil ;
Hushed now are all the harsh and jangled chords :
For a brief space there shall be sleep and silence,
Then a soft strain, and sweet and loving words.

For One speeds swiftly to the unknown region,
Who " in this harsh world drew his breath in pain."
" The rest is silence."   But in calm and sunshine
May not earth's storm-bent blossoms lift their heads
    again ?

V.

"JUDITH SHAKESPEARE."

(A' REMINISCENCE).

Inscribed respectfully to MR. WILLIAM BLACK.

I.

THROUGH a fair land she wanders,
 Wrapped in a golden dream ;
Where through green meadows glideth
 Our England's dearest stream :

Or, where in woods' recesses,
 The "dim sweet" violets blow,
While to the budding branches
 The breezes murmur low.

The day is "filled with music" ; ·
 Glamour is all around :
And in her quiet chamber
 Still floats the magic sound :

There, the first sunrays softly
 Creep through the lattice bars ;
Or clinging ivy maketh
 A leaf-frame for the stars.

And, crown of all the beauty,
   There springs a wondrous flower—
A Rose of fragrant blooming—
   Within this Maiden's bower!

Know, (would ye learn the secret
   Of such a mighty spell)
Miranda must dream sweetly
   In Prosper's magic cell!

II.

Closed is the Maiden's casement;
   No song the house doth fill:
Round the forsaken arbour
   The weeds grow up at will.

The sunshine all hath vanished
   That once so brightly shone;
For the dear Rose she cherished
   Is " from her garden gone ";

And one beside her pillow
   Watches a dying flame:
From heights of fame and glory
   To that still couch he came.

In a far heavenly city
   Swing back the shining gates—
Here in a shadowed chamber
   The white-veiled Angel waits.

Before his awful Presence
　　The elves and fairies flee ;
And even the harp of Ariel
　　Dare wake no melody.

He calls the Maiden gently :
　　She may not halting stand,
But with slow wistful footsteps
　　Follows the beckoning Hand.

III.

But, see ! while Angels welcome her
　　And in glad song rejoice ;
She pauses near the portal bright
　　Hearing an earthly voice.

One writes that Love may conquer Death
　　With might more strong and sweet ;
And in his love that stays her steps
　　The whole world's heart doth beat !

So she, to bless dear earth again
　　Descends the mystic stair—
In her sweet eyes the light of Heaven,
　　Its gleam upon her hair.

Miranda's loving feet once more
　　Enter the magic cell ;
Till Prosper breaks his staff of might
　　In that dear spot to dwell.

Once more the elves and fairy sprites
    Dance in the moon's soft ray,
And with "quaint Ariel" at their head
    Resume their ancient sway.

The wondrous Rose blooms rich again ;
    Its grace shall ne'er depart ;
For, evermore this happy Maid
    Wears it upon her heart !

VI.

THE WAKING.

"Beautiful Evelyn Hope is dead."—R. BROWNING.

SEE! she has kept your token,
  You remember what you said?
Wait! the green leaf is withered :
  She will give you now instead

Her heart, a bright red blossom,
  That in shade and quiet grew ;
No bud with close-shut petals—
  ·Flower of spirit, flame and dew.

You deemed her far above you,
  That Evelyn of sixteen years ;
She lay so white and silent,
  Heeding not your hopes and fears.

Your heart's voice then she heard not,
  Nor in speech replied that day ;
Now the leaf its secret telleth,
  Hearken what her sweet tones say !

Your love saw hope beyond you,
　　As it gleamed, a distant star :
Say now, as the glory brightens,
　　Was it ever faint and far?

She lay at sunset sleeping,
　　Your leaf in her sweet cold hands :
With dawn her soul hath wakened ;
　　She remembers and understands !

VII.

THE ANGEL'S ANSWER.

See R. Browning's "*Guardian Angel.*"

O STRONG sweet voicéd singer, with brow by thought
    expanded,
In labour high and noble many fleeting years have
    sped
Since that bright day at Fano, when from Guercino's
    canvas
The beauty of his Angel o'er thy soul like balm was
    shed !

There, as thou breath'dst thy prayer in soft and
    measured cadence,
Sweet as the low-toned murmur of the wavelets on
    the beach,
Was not in living beauty the Angel hovering near
    thee,
Though of such gracious Presence there might not be
    sign or speech ?

Has thou not heard full often, when thy right hand of
    cunning
Wakened to mighty music the sweet harp's echoing
    string,

Still ever and anon through earth's din and discord
stealing
The Guardian Angel's whisper, the soft sweep of his
strong wing?

Yea! doth he still not linger, until one day his coming
Shall end for thee for ever all of pain below the skies;
And the hand, whose quiet pressure lays to sleep all
sorrow,
Be laid for health and soothing tenderly upon thine
eyes?

Thus then, as once thou pray'dst, shall God's dear
Angel guide thee;
Bid thee in soft-toned accents lay each earthly burthen
down;
And thy dearest boon, perchance, where "love," in
truth, "is duty,"
Shall be the pure and gentle love that was thy. earth-
life's crown.

And if then *thou* shouldest, as again his bright sphere
leaving,
In all his white-winged glory he stoopeth to thy side,
And the door of Paradise thou seest for thee stand
open,
A moment turn thine eyes away, thy Angel shall not
chide!

May 7th, 1888.

F

VIII.

SPRING DAWN.

"Lo, the Winter is past."

ABOVE the hills the sun glints softly :
    Tender light is in the skies :
In verdant hollows safely sheltered
    The flock yet slumbering lies.

What promise fair of summer glory
    In the East now shines afar !
And in the wood's dim twilight gleaming,
    See ! the first faint primrose star.

Now all green blades with new life kindle,
    Overswept by spring's soft breeze,
Which whispers still of bloom and fruitage
    To the buds upon the trees.

Soon each dark pine in forest standing,
    Clad in robe of tender green,
May well forget in new-found beauty
    All bare boughs that may have been.

Through old Earth's heart a thrill is passing :
    Soon will wake her sleeping seeds ;
And she, for fairest bridal raiment,
    Will put off her mourning weeds.

E'en those low mounds, where wayworn pilgrims
    Lie so still on breast of Earth,
Made bright with flowers to new life risen,
    Preach not Death, but wondrous Birth.

Easter Day, *1888.*

IX.

NOCTURNE.

(FROM THE GERMAN).

On the steep hill's summit standing
  As fared the sun to rest,
I saw the forest's greenness
  In gold of evening drest.

Shed from fair clouds of heaven
  Soft dew fell peacefully;
The sweet-toned bells of even
  Rang nature's lullaby.

I spake—" O heart so restless
  Unto this sweet spell yield,
And lay to sleep thy sorrow
  Like each child of the field!"

Each bright and fragrant blossom
  Doth now its sweet eyes close;
With scarcely ruffled bosom
  The brooklet softly flows.

Within a leaf-fold crinkled
  Now the tired elf doth keep ;
While on the reed dew-sprinkled
  The firefly falls asleep.

The gold-winged beetle slumbers,
  Rocked on the rose's breast :
Both weary flock and shepherd
  Seek now their place of rest.

In dewy clover meadow
  The lark her nest doth find ;
The forest's woven shadow
  Shelters the roe and hind.

The peasant in his cabin
  Is now of rest full fain ;
A dream brings back each wanderer
  To fatherland again.

Ah ! midst this peace of nature
  Deep longings fill my breast,
That I might, upward soaring,
  Reach Home this hour of rest !

X.

THE PRISONER'S SONG.

(FROM THE ITALIAN).

O BRIGHT-WINGED Swallow, sweet and fleet,
    Thou comest back each morn,
And to my dungeon, low and dark,
    Thy plaintive wail is borne.
What means the piteous strain thou dost repeat,
Tell me once more, O Swallow, sweet and fleet?

Swallow, art thou forgotten, too,
    Forsaken by thy mate?
Widowed art thou and left forlorn,
    Like me, disconsolate?
Then, well may our laments and wailings meet
In one sad minor, Swallow, fleet and sweet!

Yet, Swallow, hast thou solace left:
    Swift pinions bear thee still
Lightly to seek the faithless one
    O'er lake, and vale, and hill;
Free air, not prison bars, thy bright wings beat,
Calling him ever, Swallow, sweet and fleet!

Could I as thou! . . but this forbids—
    A low and narrow cell,
Where never sun-ray or soft breeze
    May tales of summer tell.
Where this sad plaint, uttered in pain and heat,
Reaches thee faintly, Swallow, fleet and swift!

But swift draw near the autumn days,
    When thou wilt cross the strand
To greet new seas and mountain heights
    In a fair far-off land.
Still shalt thou there thy plaintive strain repeat—
Thy pilgrim song, O Swallow, sweet and fleet!

Then for thee each drear winter morn
    My tear-dimmed eyes shall seek,
Till through the silence of the snow
    I think I hear thee speak ;
Coming once more my solitude to greet
With pitying lay, O Swallow, fleet and sweet !

When spring-tide brings thee once again,
    A cross will mark this spot ;
Rest thy tired wings upon its arms,
    It shall reproach thee not.
For then at last, dear Swallow, sweet and fleet,
Thy vesper hymns shall tell how sleep is sweet !

XI.

THE DEAD LARK

AH ! dead amongst his clover blooms
    The stricken warbler lies ;
Never again in joyous flight
    To cleave the sunny skies.

Are these thy wings, once swift and light,
    That droop so heavily ;
Could this rent bosom e'er pour forth
    A " rain of melody " ?

This morning, sunward in delight
    Thou soar'dst, a winged song.
Nor dreamt that in God's happy world
    Any would do thee wrong.

A click ! a flash ! In sudden pain
    Thy life and song both die ;
And thou art but a mangled form
    That heedless feet pass by.

Say ! Is it envy of their song
    Or of their soaring wings
That moves the ruthless hand to slay
    God's " happy living things " ?

Methinks they might have left in peace
    A little brown bird's nest,
Nor with their deadly weapon stilled
    The music of thy breast!

Ah, skylark sweet! men are too base
    Celestial strains to heed,
Or surely, such a song as thine
    Had earned a better meed!

Why didst thou not in cloudland stay,
    Or soar away to Heaven,
Where Angels, better taught than men,
    Prize gifts that God hath given?

XII.

TO THE LITTLE BIRDS IN MY GARDEN.

(FROM THE ITALIAN).

Dear little birds, so gay and free !
    That still on joyous wing,
As dawns God's light in a new day,
    Glad songs of welcome sing :

The harmony of this sweet hour
    Within your hearts is shed ;
While through the ever brightening sky
    Joy with your song is spread.

Dear little birds, our Father's care !
    Methinks 'twere little wrong
To hold my mother's gentle faith
    That prayer is in your song ?

Surely it is a sacred thing
    Amidst sin's ruin set,
Lest the pure joy of upward flight
    The world should quite forget !

XIII.

THE RAINBOW.

(FROM THE GERMAN).

WHERE each bright rainbow touches earth
  There gleams a cup of gold,
And whoso finds the magic spot
  Its brightness may behold.

Brimming within the golden cup
  Sparkles bright wine of Heaven,
And from all lips the draught that drain
  Thirst is for ever driven.

By day and night the gleam to gain
  I sought the wide world round ;
But never came to any land
  Where rainbows reach the ground.

Never I found in any land
  The golden wine-cup filled,
And the long thirst that burns my heart
  Will not be quenched or stilled.

XIV.

TO THE STARS.

(FROM THE GERMAN).

STARS! In the heaven's blue distance,
 That upon our twilight rise;
And, celestial radiance shedding,
 Earthward bend with angel eyes,
Do not your sweet and gracious beams bid strife and
 pain depart,
And breathe the blessed peace of Heaven into our
 storm-tossed heart?

Stars! In your far blue distance
 Do they dream life's fleeting dream?
Do they feel the pangs or pleasures
 That we joy or sorrow deem?
Still may the spirit sigh with grief, or thrill with deep
 delight,
Beyond the narrow sunlit space that bounds our
 earthly sight?

Stars! In the far blue distance
 E'en now as ye softly shine,
Ye shed from your far-off glory
 A promise of peace Divine,

Will ye not then one day from your golden pastures
    bend,
And let your perfect calm and rest on weary souls
    descend ?

      Stars, in the far blue distance !
        Till my spirit breaks its chains,
      And with swift eager pinion
        Soareth to your peaceful plains,
With yearning hope and steadfast faith I lift my eyes
    to you :
O Stars, so sweet, and pure, and fair, your message
    must be true !

XV.

THE LAST SWALLOW.

YES, Sweet : the summer's fair long days are over,
　　The western wind blows cold ;
E'en in the dim depths of the sheltered woodland
　　Fast fades rich autumn's gold.

No more on bright fleet wing the flashing swallows
　　Gleam in a sunlit sky :
One only—last of our dear summer heralds—
　　Lingers to say good-bye.

Why dost thou follow his swift flight so fondly
　　With wistful tender eyes ?
Will he bear thy heart away with him, O maiden,
　　To the sunny southern skies ?

Bare winter comes.　Close folded in Earth's bosom
　　Each gentle flower will sleep ;
And thy sweet eyes, O Love, will ache with watching
　　When the snow lies white and deep.

Then, never let thy heart forget the springtime
    Through winter dark and long ;
For, surely, from its chill and barren silence
    Shall break at length a song !

Are not two Angels, Faith and Hope, still left thee
    To soothe thy hour of pain ?—
When the first swallow comes with spring's glad
        greeting,
    He shall bring Love again !

Christmas, 1889.

XVI.

"IRIS."

A TWILIGHT face, where light and shade
    Meet as in summer skies :
Like star-gleams in deep silent pools
    The soul-light in her eyes.

Sweet lips that keep like crimson buds
    Their secret yet untold :
Hair like the dusky wing of Night
    Just touched with Morning's gold.

A voice which, as a tremulous harp
    When wandering winds sweep by,
Breathes forth in tones to hold men mute
    The soul's deep melody.

One in whose presence care seems light,
    Earth-mists are backward rolled ;
And once again our tired hearts dream
    The Angel-dreams of old.

XVII.

THE FATE OF A FLOWER.

(A CONCEIT).

I.

A PROUD, sweet, purple lily
  Grew by the river's edge,
Among the reeds and grasses
  And ragged broken sedge.

The velvet leaves lie sleeping,
  Close-wrapped in bright green sheath,
Till the Spring-Spirit passes
  And wakes them with soft breath.

Ah, then the winds and sunbeams
  A royal sight behold ;
The purple petals open
  And show a heart of gold !

Now all the fragrant blossoms
  Joy in a queen so fair ;
And even the reeds and sedges
  The same sweet burden bear.

The wild and free Wind-Spirit
  Lingers the Flower to greet,
With soft caressing touches
  And whispers low and sweet.

The birds with joyous trilling
  Seem still to sing its praise ;
And all around is brightness
  In those fair summer days.

II.

A many-tinted Dragon-Fly
  Flew by on burnished wing :
The Lily saw the dazzling sheen,
  But recked not of the sting.

Deep-piercing through its golden heart,
  The cruel thirsty Fly
Spared not the purple cup to drain ;
  Then left the Flower to die.

Its royal raiment soiled and rent,
  It lies among the weeds :
The birds still warble, but the *Wind*
  Sighs in the bending reeds.

XVIII.

TO MY BROTHER PERCIVAL.

THERE are who tell us old romance is fable ;
  King Arthur but a poet's idle dream ;
That chivalry hath from the world quite vanished—
  A passing golden gleam.

Surely soul-blindness, born of earth and Mammon,
  Bids men embrace a creed so cold and bare :
Not yet, methinks, "dissolved the *whole* Round Table,"
  Its deeds and glories rare !

Nay : but while one, true, pure, high-souled, unselfish,
  Doth 'mid our dark and tangled earth-ways tread,
Bearing a Knight's name in an unstained scutcheon,
  The old Knights are not dead !

October 24th, 1888.

XIX.

HID TREASURE.

(FROM THE ITALIAN).

'Tis night, and the "vexed Sea," of rest deprived,
    Climbs to the sky above ;
And strives with waves that ceaseless foam and toss
    To reach the Moon his Love.

In vain he tries that giddy height to scale—
    A fond and fruitless quest ;
Ah, foolish One ! canst thou then not perceive
    Her light in thine own breast ?

Doth not thy Love, from thee though far away,
    In thy heart prisoned lie ?
What boots it then if in material form
    She stoop not from the sky ?

XX.

LINES.

(FROM THE FRENCH).

O COME, when on my couch I sleeping lie,
As Laura once to gladden Petrarch's heart,
Let thy breath touch me as thou passest by
      With a swift sigh
      My lips shall part!

Let thy glance, shining as a fair star's beam,
Shed o'er my troubled brain its gracious light,
Where ends, perchance, a long and hateful dream
      With the swift gleam
      My sleep grows bright!

Upon my lips, where love God pure doth make,
Trembles like flame, then softly drop thy kiss,
And no more Angel, Woman's aspect take . .
      In what swift bliss
      My soul shall wake!

XXI.

THE LITTLE SHROUD.

(FROM THE GERMAN).

THE little Baby died.
Ah! how the Mother wept!
Watching by day and night,
For tears she hath not slept.

*   *   *   *   *

The Babe came back, a shadowy form,
   All pale, in death-robe drest:
It plaintive speaks: "Ah, Mother mine,
   Lay thyself down to rest!
See how my little garment drips
   With tears thy love doth weep,
Sweet Mother, in so cold a shroud
   Thy Baby cannot sleep."

*   *   *   *   *

The gentle Vision disappears,
The weeping Mother dries her tears.

XXII.

CIRCE.

" Dusk-haired and gold-robed, o'er the golden wine
    She stoops, wherein, distilled of death and shame,
    Sink the black drops ; while, lit with fragrant flame,
Round her spread board the golden sunflowers shine."—
                                    D. G. ROSSETTI.

YES,   She is very fair.   Men learn it but too surely :
    Sweet are her eyes and deep ; from her red lips soft
        words,
Distilled like honey drop ; yet bleeding hearts bear
        witness
    How that they oft may wound and pierce as very
        swords.

Her baleful loveliness, born not of earth or Heaven,
    Is of those Hateful Ones whose steps draw nigh to
        Hell :
Those once within her toils she follows unrelenting
    And ever round them weaves her dark and fatal
        spell.

Before her sons of men pour forth in full libation
    The gifts that God bestows most precious and
        divine :
She treads them in the dust ; and then, with scorn
        and loathing,
    Offers them in return her draughts of deadly wine.

Yea : oftentimes she cometh vested as an Angel,
  And with enchanting voice doth as a siren sing :
She snareth victims fast ; nor, till her net enfolds
    them,
  Hear they in her sweet song the tones of mockery
    ring.

Full are her lavish hands of gifts that seem most
    goodly.
  Fair doth she promise bliss it ne'er was hers to give :
Her fruit is that of Sodom, bitterness and ashes,
  Whereof man never yet was found to taste and live.

Yet doth she reign—a Queen, enthroned in might and
    splendour—
  Leading earth's noblest children captive at her will :
And we who see oft ask, with hearts perplexed and
    doubting,
  Why hidden under beauty lie snares the soul that
    kill ?

Yet God is still above, and from all things He fashioned
  His Hand shall surely sweep all trace of ill away ;
Then in a fair new world, where all is as it seemeth,
  Beauty and goodness shall be one that day !

XXIII.

PAOLO AND FRANCESCA.

(A PICTURE BY G. F. WATTS).

Dante. Inferno v.

BEHOLD these Spirits who in robes of mourning
   Cleave with swift wings Hell's thick and noisome air,
No light of hope in their sad faces kindles,
   Grey with the ashen colour of despair!
In earth's sweet light erewhile they walked in pleasure,
   Seeing the fair sun rise, the pale stars shine
Until the fatal hour that lit a flame unholy—
   Look in their faces and behold the sign!
Still bound together fast by links unhallowed,
   For their lost peace these anguished Spirits yearn;
For flames that seem on earth to warm and lighten
   In Hell have power only to sear and burn.
From memory or hope no comfort may they borrow,
Their only solace, "sorrow's crown of sorrow!"

XXIV.

"TILL DEATH."

THEY met and parted. (God in Heaven shall judge
    All souls He made one day.)
  The fair spring sky above them glowing
    Seemed turned from blue to grey.

Why must their lips pour forth to pierce and rend
    Words like envenomed darts,
  Yet all the while a peace unspoken
    Is nestling at their hearts?

O'er each heart lies close-drawn a shadowing veil,
    Between them walls of ice:
  Could it lift or thaw a moment,
    Behind is paradise!

But Pride bars the way with a sword that flames;
    And now through all the years
  Hope gives place to a passionate yearning
    And searching with bitter tears.

Cold falls the rain and slow from leaden clouds;
    Set is the sun at noon:
  The air is filled with sounds of wailing;
    Lost seems life's dearest boon.

Henceforth they tread in aching hopeless pain
    With weary bleeding feet,
  Paths that lie close, yet far are sundered,
    Lines which may never meet.

Yet Hope lives! See, an Angel draweth near—
    A King who endeth strife :
  An olive branch he bears for sceptre,
    And Death gives more than Life!

XXV.

WANDERER'S SONG.

(FROM THE GERMAN).

WHEN long shadows from the mountains
 Stretch darkly o'er the sea,
Then the heart, thrilled with sweet sorrow,
 Looks backward longingly.

When in flocks the snowy seamews
 Fly shorewards o'er the main,
Then a faithful heart's calm shelter
 I seek to ease my pain.

Glad and gay, in morning sunshine,
 The wanderer loves to roam :
Ever still as fall the shadows
 The heart will sigh for home.

XXVI.

A LOOSED CORD.

I.

TOGETHER in a dream of bliss
    We trod the woodland ways ;
Methought that Nature's very heart
    Seemed throbbing with your praise.

The sun-rays touched you, artist-wise,
    And painted, unaware,
Light in your dark eyes' liquid deeps,
    Gold in your dusky hair.

Hope sang that day from every bough,
    And glowed in every flower ;
We walked no more on earth-paths old
    But in lost Eden's bower.

II.

What voice, more sweet than earth's love-tones,
    Hath laid you thus to sleep,
And hushed the music of your speech
    To silence long and deep ?

What kiss upon your rose-sweet lips
    Hath left them pale and cold ;
And bade your eyes like mist-veiled stars
    Their light a secret hold ?

What touch hath stilled your heart's quick pulse ;
    And crossed, in marble rest,
The hands love's pressure could not hold
    Thus meekly on your breast ?

III.

Ah, Sweet, a Love more deep than mine
    Hath bent you to Its Will :—
For this, with lilies o'er you strewn,
    You lie so white and still.

A seal, by God's own Hand impressed,
    Is on your quiet brow ;
No furrow born of care or pain
    May mar its beauty now.

Let it be so.   The love and faith
    You gave, are mine to keep :
More than I could, God loved you, Sweet,
    And so you fell asleep.

XXVII.

ALTERNATIONS.

(FROM THE GERMAN).

THE autumn wind wails through the forest
  Already the swallows are flown :
How soon stand the trees bare and lifeless,
  Ah ! how soon, Sweet, the summer is gone !

Ere spring's fair blooms scarce have unfolded,
  Scarce budded the rose in May,
And love in the young heart scarce wakened ;
  The leaves fall, and—all passes away.

Our love and delight, care and sorrow,
  All swift as a dream's shadows fly :
What is left to us, Sweet, when day closes ?
  Can we answer with aught save a sigh ?

Yet where this rose now breathes its perfume,
  Next year one as fragrant may wave ;
And the vows of two hearts full as loving
  Be whispered one day o'er our grave !

XXVIII.

LIFE, DEATH AND LOVE.

I.

A VIGIL spent in darkness, in deep gloom and heavy
  night—
A grey cold sky at dawning, a flush of rosy light—

A burst of waking sunlight, and such grace to life is
  given
That each dark vale and barren peak gleams with the
  gold of heaven.

With all the old sweet glamour Love is weaving
  Eden's bowers,
And glorious show on Life's fair Tree the red and
  glowing flowers.

Swept by Love's light swift wing the heart thrills like
  a trembling lyre,
And its harmony seems echoed by a hidden heavenly
  choir.

II.

Just the passing of an Angel, the shadow of its wing,
And bare and silent winter follows one day of spring.

The silver string is loosened ; the harp's sweet music
    mute ;
And hanging on Life's blasted Tree dead leaves for
    golden fruit.

III.

Yet may the mute harp wake again to sweeter melody ;
And a new spring make fair once more the bare and
    blasted Tree.

Though Death a while may triumph, Love still doth
    reign a King,
And o'er the Grave's grim trophies hovers Psyche's
    radiant wing !

XXIX.

MUSIC IN DEATH.

(FROM THE FRENCH).

FRIENDS, would ye aid me in my hour of anguish,
　　Let speech in silence die!
But let soft music round me linger,
　　Stilling death's agony.

The heart by music's tone is soothed and lifted
　　Till Heaven's own chant is heard—
Therefore, O Friends, I will that music waken,
　　But speak to me no word.

No more of harsh, perplexing words.　My spirit,
　　Nearing the "Silent Land,"
Cares but for sounds that to the heart speak softly,
　　Too tired to understand.

Let such a strain as bathes the soul in rapture
　　Come, with its magic breath,
And draw me gently from life's fierce delirium
　　Through a sweet dream to death!

XXX.

LOVE'S PATIENCE.

I CARE not that in days of joy and sunshine
    Thy heart should turn to me :
Wait till the song hath ceased, the sheaves are gar-
    nered,
    No leaf is on the tree.

I would not lay upon a young life's gladness
    The shadow of my years ;
Nor mar the music of thy soul's blithe singing
    With sound of falling tears.

I ask not now to see my hope's fruition ;
    I am content to wait :
One day, I know, back on its tardy hinges
    Will swing the golden gate ;

And we into the golden Land of Promise
    Shall enter hand in hand ;
My heart will whisper then its happy secret,
    And thou wilt understand !

XXXI.

REQUIESCAT.

SLEEP! with the kiss of Azrael upon thine eyes
    Each throb of pain to heal ;
Never shall any light from earthly skies
    Break that enduring seal.

Sleep! for the veiléd Angel peace with him doth
      bring—
    The sun slants to the west :
Then shrink not if beneath his dark-plumed wing
    He fold thee to his breast.

His voice is solemn ; on his brow, sad as a dream,
    No joyous smile appears :
The gems that on his sombre vesture gleam
    Are bitter human tears.

Amid the sons of men he walks with soundless tread,
    God's Messenger unseen ;
Yet oft his touch upon a pain-racked head
    A welcome thing hath been.

Sleep! for the watch he keeps in dim and silent night
    Lasts but a little space ;
Another Angel of excelling might
    Waiteth to take his place.

His robes are radiant ; as from Heaven's portal
    Light o'er his path is shed :
Earth's fairest flowers, made by his touch immortal,
    He wreathes about his head.

With all fair fruits he sowed for his own reaping
    His gracious hands are filled :
Each wail of pain and sound of human weeping
    Is at his whisper stilled.

Then sleep : and to thy sealéd eyes be given
    Visions of joy and bliss,
Till, bending o'er thee with the smile of Heaven,
    Love wakes thee with *his* kiss !

XXXII.

MY LITTLE SISTER

(FROM THE GERMAN).

LITTLE Sister, whom with child-tales
    Once I sung to sleep;
The sweeter Angels now have lulled thee
    Into rest more deep!

Little Sister, thou didst slumber,
    To wake where tempests cease:
Farewell! we still are midst the breakers,
    Thou in the Port of Peace!

XXXIII.

FLOWER-DE-LUCE.

SWEET Flower, the praise of all Earth's fairest
    children
    To thee were scanty meed ;
Yet bend to-day and hear, low-breathed and tender,
    A message from the reed !—

"Most dear of all dear flowers God's hand hath
    planted,"
    Well may my spirit deem
An Angel led me to the place of blessing
    Where thy fair petals gleam !

"Thou cam'st, O Flower of Light, a Heaven-sent
    Herald "
    To cheer the hour of gloom ;
And with the gracious sweetness of thy presence
    To bid the desert bloom !

Now, filled with nectar of thy purple chalice,
    My heart deep joy receives ;
Therefore, my Flower, with love's best benediction,
    I kiss thy fragrant leaves.

God send thee, while thou makest fair Earth's garden,
      The softest of His showers ;
Then plant thee by the quiet streams of Eden
      Among His choicest flowers ;

And grant thee, where the bands of white-winged
      Angels
      Gather around His Feet,
The smile wherein all Earth and Heaven's best sun-
      shine
      In perfect concord meet !

January 5th, 1888.

XXXIV.

WHEN THE LEAVES FALL .

(FROM THE ITALIAN).

WHEN the leaves fall, and my low grave
    Thou seek'st in hallowed ground—
A quiet nook where green boughs wave
    And blossoms spring around—
Then linger, ere from that still place
    Thy loving steps depart,
And gather, thy dark locks to grace,
    These flowers born of my heart !
They are my songs that unsung died away—
Those words of love I found not voice to say.

PART III

MISCELLANEOUS POEMS.

ALL' PIÙ CARA.

O'ER thee, in all its fulness,
  Descend the Holy Breath
That bade the Lily blossom
  In lowly Nazareth !

His peace, Who from the stable,
  Where in low crib He lay,
Put all earth's strife to silence,
  Enfold thy heart to-day !

Till, in the Many Mansions,
  All toil and sorrow ends,
Our Father be thy Keeper,
  His Angels be thy friends !

Christmas Eve, 1889.

I.

LENT LILIES.

"Consider the lilies of the field."—*S. Matt.*, vi. 28.

PALE tender blooms, not yours such hues
    As theirs that once of yore
In more than regal glory dressed
    Adorned Gennesaret's shore.

Ye rise while still the bleak winds blow
    Fair from your chill dark bed,
Though o'er you pallid Northern skies
    For Eastern blue be spread.

Ye spring, ere earth hath scarcely doffed
    Her mantle cold and white,
And gather in your golden cups
    All that ye may of light.

Sure He, who from the Eastern flowers
    His holy lessons drew,
Bids us who would His teaching heed
    Regard these lilies too.

K

For in the garden of His grace
 He souls as flowers doth tend,
And there all tints, or bright or pale,
 In harmony may blend.

There some, in royal purple robed,
 The martyr's colours bear ;
And some, His lilies wan and sweet,
 A paler garment wear.

Yet all these blossoms of His hand
 The Gardener's love doth bless ;
And for each one the garb He gives
 Is its own fitting dress.

All have received His quickening showers,
 O'er all His sun hath shone ;
And His own hand one day shall cull
 The plants Himself hath sown.

Then, in one perfect garland twined,
 Its beauty each shall yield
When with pale Lenten blooms He binds
 Bright " lilies of the field."

II.

TWO CROWNS.

DESPISED and scorned, in mocking purple drest,
  Christ wore a crown of pain,
That we through His long agony might rest
  And crowns eternal gain.

Now crowned with glory in the Heaven's height,
  By God the Father's side,
He wields the sceptre of all-conquering might—
  Who liveth, and hath died.

Henceforth two crowns He beareth on His Brow,
  A mingled diadem ;
And every thorn that pierced and rent is now
  In beauty like a gem.

Henceforth, for those who follow where He led,
  No pang shall be in vain,
Since light from His triumphal crown is shed
  Upon their crowns of pain.

III.

SUNSET HYMN.

FATHER, Who hath taught us
    That sweet Name to say,
Thy sure love hath brought us
    To the close of day!

Thou to us hast given
    All we have of good,
E'en Thy Son from Heaven
    Sparing not the Rood.

JESU, full of pity,
    Succour to us send,
From their golden City
    While Thine Angels bend!

Thou hast known each sorrow
    Human hearts may bear,
Who from us didst borrow
    Robe of flesh to wear.

SPIRIT, pure and loving,
　　In Thy might draw near,
From our souls removing
　　All that makes us fear!

Where Thy wing doth hover
　　All is pure and bright,
Grant us that safe cover
　　Through the hours of night.

Now dark shades have found us,
　　Day no more we see,
With Thy love surround us,
　　Blessed Trinity!

Amen

IV.

THE CHILDREN'S BLESSING.

(SUGGESTED).

"They brought young children to Him . . . and He
put His hands upon them and blessed them."

S. Mark, x. 13, 16.

"Through laying on of hands the Holy Ghost was given."
Acts viii. 18.

HATH He then left us orphans
Who for Judah's children cared,
Are we debarred the blessing
That they once with gladness shared?

Must we, who to the Saviour
By His Cross are brought so nigh,
Raise for His benediction
An exceeding bitter cry?

Nay : Christ, Who on the children
Once in blessing laid His hands,
Christ, Who is with us always,
Now before His Altar stands ;

And richer blessing crowneth
Gentile children when they kneel,
And God's own hand endows them
With the Spirit's Holy Seal.

Then be the vows breathed softly,
Vows they cannot choose but pay,
Echoing the earlier promise
Of each blest baptismal day!

Be God's Voice heard above them,
As He from His glory bends,
And each meek soul that seeks Him
With His heavenly grace defends!

Thus made His own for ever,
Endued with sevenfold might,
They will set their stedfast faces
Towards the shining of God's light.

And sure as faithful soldiers
They may never fail to stand
Whom our Father dowers thus richly
With the strength of His Right Hand!

February 3rd, 1889.

V.

SHUTTING OUT THE LAMBS.

S. Luke, xvii. 2.

OUTSIDE the fold in sin and darkness stráying,
    With fleeces torn and stained,
The flock that should have drunk the living waters
    And the green pastures gained !

Are these the lambs for whom the faithful Shepherd
    Endured the Cross and shame—
Those lambs for whom His soul in anguish travailed,
    Those whom He calls by name?

The little ones, on whom in pity gazing
    Perchance His eyes grew dim ;
Whom knowing well the perils that beset them
    He bade us bring to Him ?

Yes : these are they whom, faithless hireling shepherds,
    We starved, who should have fed ;
Whom, when they hungered sore for heavenly know-
        ledge,
    We gave a stone for bread.

Are earthly pathways, then, such easy treading,
 That in our sinful pride
We dared withhold the blessed light God giveth
 The little feet to guide?

Surely not *theirs* the blame if to the tempter
 They fell an easy prey,
And left, for paths that end in shame and sorrow,
 The safe and narrow way.

Let *us* take heed, lest on our failing vision
 Pale forms of children rise,
With little hands outstretched in piteous pleading
 And sad reproachful eyes;

Lest through our fault the little souls Christ ransomed
 Sin's robe of sorrow wear;
Lest little lips we never taught to praise Him
 An awful witness bear,

As on our ears in all its woe and terror
 Falls the dread word, " Too late,"
And round our neck in righteous retribution
 Is hung the " millstone's " weight!

VI.

S. COLUMBA.

June 9th (Scotch Kalendar).

S. Columba left Ireland, A.D. 565, to preach to the Picts in the Scottish Highlands. He settled in Iona, a rocky island three miles south of Staffa, and there built a church and monastery, which became a centre of learning and education. Here he laboured until A.D. 595, when he died at the age of 77 years, and was buried in the monastery which he had founded. One of his favourite occupations seems to have been that of transcribing copies of the Gospels and other parts of Holy Scripture; and his biographer records that he was overtaken by death while engaged in copying the 34th Psalm.

A DOVE from Christ's own Ark sent forth
  The stormy wave to breast,
Columba to the Western Isles
  Doth bear His message blest.

Where nature's voices harsh and wild
  Their concert never cease,
He plants amid the roar and strife
  An olive branch of peace.

By grace of God so thrived and grew
  The holy seed he bore,
That soon a garden of the Lord
  Smiles on the wave-gashed shore.

The Voice that once bade blessed John
    In lonely Patmos write,
Now bids Columba's rocky isle
    Hold forth the word of light.

Long years with faithful voice and pen
    He laboured for his Lord,
Till, borne one day on June's soft breath,
    There came a sweeter word ;

And then, like dove that sinks to rest
    With song at sunset calm,
God's sleep stole o'er him while he penned
    Lines of the holy Psalm.

Did not the Angel of the Lord
    Still tarry round his way,
And draw with smile of heavenly love
    More near at close of day,

And upward bear the saint of God,
    Where—rich and sweet reward !—
In fuller bliss he tastes and sees
    How gracious is the Lord ?

VII.

A NEW YEAR'S BLESSING.

May He upon the Rood Who died
Draw thee, Belovéd, to His side!

May He Who trod our earthly ways
Uphold thy footsteps all the days!

Thy shield be God Who reigns above,
Thy shelter His eternal love!

Though earthly loves may pass or fail,
That star for thee grow nèver pale

Till, for thee from the Blesséd Land
Shall bend a loving Angel band,

And, gathered to the Saviour's breast,
Toil is no more, but most sweet rest!

New Year's Eve, 1889.

VIII.

THE SILENT MONK.

(FOUNDED ON AN OLD LEGEND).

" AH ! why dost thou, O Brother, ne'er, as it still is
    meet,
Uplift thy voice in praise unto our Lord most sweet ? "

Thus day by day the Monks within their cloister wall
Upon the Silent Brother cease not still to call.

The slow sands many years drop silent through Time's
    glass,
But never word of praise that Brother's lips did pass.

In Compline Psalm his voice no note would ever raise :
In Vesper anthem never swell the chant of praise.

At length through his dim. cell a veiléd Form doth
    steal,
And sets on those still lips a more enduring seal.

Loud wail the Monks, " Alas ! the day of praise is o'er ;
Our silent Brother now hath power to sing no more."

" Can any power avail speech from dead lips to win ? "
Ah, deaf ears that had missed the strains that stirred
    within !

With such sad speech they bear and lay him low to
    rest ;
Nor dream that who is silent sometimes singeth best.

But see ! from that dark mound wherein the Dead
    they lay
A gracious lily springs to greet the new-born day.

Fair shine the clustered leaves, meet for an Angel's
    bower,
And fair the blossoms gleam of blessed Mary's flower.

No more a fountain sealed, from that still heart up-
    springs
Praise that the Angels hear, and stay with folded
    wings.

Amazed the Monks draw near a sight so strange to
    see,
And whisper, "Sure this must a Heaven-sent token
    be."

Now mute themselves, they learn, their eyes all dim
    with tears,
The secret, wondrous sweet, of those long silent years,

When, as with God's own hand in Pentecostal flame,
They read on each white leaf inscribed the Holy Name!

IX.

LIGHT IN SHADOW.

THE Curse hath made earth dreary,
   Her paths full hard to tread ;
Yet are there rays of brightness
   Upon the darkness shed.

The bramble's thorny branches
   Withhold not fruitage sweet ;
A bloom of beauty crowneth
   The thistle at our feet.

God's light 'mid autumn sadness
   Doth gild the bending sheaves ;
And, when the spring buds kindle,
   His Spirit stirs the leaves.

When, all her blossoms sleeping,
   Earth seems a barren place,
He guides the Frost-King's fingers
   Till magic flowers they trace.

Though oft, our earth mist rising,
  The heaven's pure blueness mars,
He hath not failed to scatter
  Among the clouds His stars.

Signs of His love unfailing
  We may all round us find,
Who, when His east wind bloweth,
  Still stayeth His rough wind,

That our dull hearts forget not,
  What cloud soe'er may rise,
That He Who planted Eden
  Prepareth Paradise.

X.

COUNSEL TO CROWDS.

(FROM RÜCKERT).

How closely set stand bush and tree
  The forest ways among !
How in our world the eager crowd
  Each other press and throng !

What nook soe'er or path thou fill'st,
  To that place God thee sent ;
Therefore, as snail in house of shell,
  Be in thy place content.

Art thou a rose that crowns the bush,
  Thine be it God to bless ;
Art thou but moss upon its stem,
  Then thank thy God no less !

XI.

RESURGAM.

AND is this all—
'Neath shroud and pall
Sealed lips and brow of snow,
    A mound of green,
    Where, all unseen,
The shadows come and go ?

    Was it for this
    That woe and bliss
The quivering heart-strings thrilled—
    To lie in dust,
    The brightness rust,
The God-waked music stilled?

    Ah, no ! dead grain
    That lives again,
Upspringing from the clay ;
    The sun that dies,
    Each morn to rise
And bless another day ;

The worm so mean
That still is seen
Like withered leaf to die ;
Then, a bright flower
With wings for dower,
Doth soar a butterfly :

All bid us see
The mystery
Of sleep and wondrous change,
Of Life that waits
Beyond death's gates
In glory sweet and strange.

Though, with its gleams
More swift than dreams,
Its tears that sad eyes weep,
Our " little life "
Of pain and strife
Is " rounded with a sleep ";

Yet ever round,
A mystic bound,
As sky the world above,
Doth circling lie
Eternity
And God's eternal love.

XII.

AN EASTER GREETING.

"The time of the singing of birds is come."

ONCE more doth Heaven's kiss awake the Earth
 And woo her into smiles ;
And with sweet whispers of glad Easter birth
 Her ancient grief beguiles.

Once more from her dark breast the fair flowers spring,
 As life shall spring from death,
And from their fragrant censers sunward fling
 The incense of their breath.

Well might we deem, that in the quiet night
 While Earth in slumber lay,
The Easter Angels lingering in their flight
 Had dropped them on their way.

Through wood and plain now Spring's clear music
 thrills ;
  Of joy and life it sings ;
Of mossy glades where softly flow the rills ;
  Of swallows' gleaming wings.

Fair seems old Earth as when in days of yore
      Love's light shone in her eyes ;
For through her weary heart there steals once more
      A thought of Paradise.

Yet, Love, look upward from her flower-strewn plains,
      Her blossoms " fair and frail."
To fairer realms whose sunshine never wanes,
      Where blows no wintry gale !

Dost thou not hear e'en now through each sweet tone
      A Voice more sweet than they,
That softly calls, " Awake my love ; fair one,
      Arise and come away " ?

Lo ! in the Garden Sharon's Rose doth grace
      The flowers all stay for thee :
Nor will it, till thou fillest there thy place,
      In beauty perfect be.

Easter Eve, 1889.

XIII.

A DIRGE FOR PRINCE MAMILIUS.

"A sad tale's best for winter."—*A Winter's Tale.*

SLEEP, little Prince! thy tale is told ;
    The rosy lips are still :
No listening crickets e'er again
    Shall hush their piping shrill.

Thine was indeed " A Winter's Tale,'
    Too sad for such short years—
All sweet Spring's sunshine and delight
    Quenched in a rain of tears.

Ah! that not e'en thy charms could bid
    The jealous clamour cease
That with relentless fury dared
    To " batter at thy peace."

When he who should have shielded, struck
    His consort's spotless fame,
Thy little loyal tender heart
    Broke for a mother's shame.

Now pain is past ; and o'er thy grave,
    More soft than cradle bed,
Her white plumes dipped in rainbow hues
    The wing of Hope is spread.

The Gods are just, and their slow mills
    Will one day work the right :
The " Winter's Tale " of gloom and grief
    Shall end in sunset light.

Dream then, and see, in royal robe
    One kneel with outstretched hands
Where, wrapped in beauty grave and sweet,
    A breathing statue stands !

XIV.

MACBETH.

" I have bought
Golden opinions from all sorts of people.
    *   *   *   *   *
I have supped full with horrors."

Macbeth.

No more around thee tones that praise and bless
    A golden murmur keep,
But, muttered thunder of a nearing storm,
    " Curses, not loud but deep."

Life's wine that sparkled in a golden bowl
    Is now a bitter draught,
Circean potion in Hell's cauldron seethed,
    With fear and loathing quaffed.

" Stay, ye imperfect speakers, tell me more."
    Such seed thy reaping knew :
Such was a lifted drawbridge to invite
    The hateful juggling crew.

Behind thee now, a mountain of Despair,
　　　Looms the "Eternal Past,"
And all of hope thy future ever held
　　　Is in a great gulf cast ;

A livid flood, wherein thy life's red crimes
　　　Lie in unquiet graves—
No Heaven or Hell-built bark shall ever dare
　　　Those tossing crimson waves.

Now sick at heart, thou reap'st the fatal seed
　　　That made thy life accurst,
For thou in all its hideousness dost know
　　　"By the worst mean the worst."

XV.

FROM THE "GLOBE," 1610, TO THE "LYCEUM," 1889.

AH ! for the golden days of English drama,
  When on my rush-strewn stage
Fond Thisbe's lion, *alias* Snug the joiner,
  Roared in his noble rage ;

When Moonshine, with his "small light of discretion,"
  His dog and bush did stand,
And carried, to the wonder of beholders,
  His dwelling in his hand ;

When Snout, with some roughcast and lime about him,
  Would have his audience think
That he was "Wall," and his obliging fingers
  Its crannied hole or chink.

Alas ! *sic transit.* All those charms have vanished ;
  And in your cultured age
One wall ye bring not, but a solid city
  Upon your groaning stage.

Within your boxes draped with gold and velvet
  Sublimely ye aspire,
And summon now the thunder of Olympus,
  Now, the infernal fire.

On my old boards with no elaborate mounting
  Its meed of praise was won ;
On yours, without its scenic decoration,
  What play would have a run ?

Far be it from the ghost of an old theatre
  Irreverent things to say,
But yet, methinks, sometimes the nobler substance
  To shadow may give way.

XVI.

A LOST LOVE.

WHAT cloud o'er earth's sweet face has fallen
    To blot the light away,
And give for Spring and gladsome Summer
    An endless winter day?

The hues that once shone fair and gracious,
    As Iris 'mid the rain,
With cruel glare of mocking brightness
    Now blind my eyes with pain.

The music that in hours long vanished
    As Angel's song rang clear,
Strikes now, like noise of angry clamour,
    Upon a sick man's ear.

In distant ways the feet have wandered
    I dreamed would ne'er depart:
Ah me! that even yet their echo
    Seems treading on my heart.

Dead Love, that once I deemed immortal,
    White ashes crown thy pyre:
Faith stricken lies; and Hope's chill finger
    May light not that spent fire.

XVII.

THE TORCH-WEED.

(FROM RÜCKERT).

OBERON the Elf-King dances
  With Titania his Queen ;
Surely such a dainty couple
  Out of Elf-Land ne'er was seen !

All the grasshoppers and crickets
  How they flock from near and far,
Striking up in clear-toned music
  Each his tiny sweet guitar !

See ! the Torch-weed tall and slender
  Fair upspringeth from the ground,
While in gay· and airy gambol
  All the Elfin choir dance round.

Hopping on the glowing branches
  As they circle it in glee,
Now their mischief-loving fingers
  Snatch its tapers from the tree.

Not an Elf but tries his hardest
  To put out each glittering spark,
That, with none to check their antics,
  They may gambol in the dark.

Lest Titania's stern Consort,
  Whom all Fairies own as King,
Drawing near with awesome sceptre
  Should break up their merry ring.

But the Torch-weed true and loyal,
  At high Oberon's behest,
Growing still despite the Elfins
  To shine brightly does its best.

As each naughty Fay upreaches
  To put out a lower light,
He sees not above it kindled
  A new taper full as bright.

When the morning breeze blows freshly,
  Of the Elves no trace is seen ;
Naught but a pale "ringlet" marketh
  That gay ball-room on the green.

But the Torch-weed, tall and lovely,
  Stayeth yet to tell its tale—
How the Elves strove hard to hurt it,
  How most sorely they did fail!

XVIII.

THE ROBING OF THE FOREST.

(FROM G. PFARRIUS).

AT birthtime of a Forest,
  The first that earth did see,
The Light and Air disputed
  What tint its robe should be.

" It must be like the sunshine
  Gold-beaming," said the Light.
The Air cried, " No : like heaven
  It must be azure bright."

Thus hard they strive ; and neither
  Will give his brother way
Until, with subtle meaning,
  Wise Mother-Earth doth say,

" Let both now work together,
  Let envy have no place ;
And whoso labours hardest,
  His robe the wood shall grace."

As now each brown branch showeth
  Its buds so small and white,
To deck the new-born Forest
  How strive the Air and Light !

In weaving of its garment
  Both hard at work are seen :
One blue, one yellow giveth ;
  And see, the robe is green !

XIX.

THE FAITHFUL HORSE.

(FROM J. KERNER).

COUNT Turnech (sore had been the fight)
A Kirk door reached as fell the night.

In forest shade that Kirk lay deep ;
Within its vaults a King doth sleep.

Here thought the Count to take his rest,
Nor recked the dart that pierced his breast.

The Count unloosed his good white steed ;
" Here, till I come, on soft grass feed."

Back swung the door with heavy thrill,
Then all in that deep vault was still.

The Count's hand reached the wall so cold,
And groping felt a coffin old.

" My tired limbs here in rest shall wait :
Old wood, break not beneath my weight."

M

Count Turnech stretched, and knew no fear,
His tall form on that ancient bier.

The sun above the hills rose red :
The Count came not : the Count lay dead.

Hath passed full many hundred year,
But still his good steed tarrieth near.

Where by the Kirk yet stands a stone
In moonlight pale he feeds alone.

XX.

A LOST HARVEST.

O'ER the fresh furrows that dark Shadow crept
    Who shuns the light of day :
A deed of darkness plotted while men slept—
    Love's seed was snatched away.

Henceforth for fruitage here ye seek in vain ;
    A barren plot it lies :
Ne'er shall the reapers with rich loaded wain
    Raise here their happy cries.

But one day He who bears the scythe and glass,
    Who e'er disputes Love's throne,
With unrelenting steps shall o'er it pass
    And claim it for his own.

XXI.

LAETA SORS.

"I have saved the bird in my bosom."

"Sir Hugh Percy fighting unsuccessfully for Henry VI. at Hedgely Moor, April, 1464, used this expression on feeling himself mortally wounded, in reference to the faith he had pledged to his unfortunate sovereign while so many deserted him."—*Chambers's Book of Days.*

AH, happy warrior! all the air
    With battle din is stirred,
He, 'mid the tumult, only hears
    The clear note of a bird.

At life's dear cost he held it fast
    The faith within his breast ;
Now in his hour of sorest need
    It sings his soul to rest.

The noise of strife hurts not his ears
    Who dies the " happy death,"
The war-blast sounds a homeward call
    As fails his panting breath.

With wounds that tell a glorious tale,
    A scutcheon without stain,
He passes to the plains of peace
    Victor, though lying slain.

XXII.

"RAYON DE LA LUNE."

(SUGGESTED BY A. WILLETTE'S PICTURE).

POOR, it may be ; of low and humble state :
    Yet while her lily blooms,
What happier maiden can the city show
    In all its gilded rooms ?

Ah ! that one unblest night the vestal moon,
    No more a face divine,
Smiles earthward ; but as from an alien sphere
    With mocking ray doth shine.

A hand —no Angel's—hath the lily snatched :
    Prone in the dust it lies ;
And well, if with her sullied bloom
    That hapless maid, too, dies.

XXIII.

CHARON AND THE LOVER.

(FROM THE FRENCH OF OLIVIER DE MAGNY, 17TH CENT.)

THE LOVER.   Ho! Charon, Charon, boatman of the
      infernal strand.

CHARON.   Who thus with eager haste my service
      doth demand?

THE LOVER.   Of a too faithful lover 'tis the tearful
      shade,

      Of one whose constant flame with
      naught but woe was paid.

CHARON.   What seekest thou of me?

THE LOVER.   To cross the fatal flood.

CHARON.   By whose hand art thou slain?

THE LOVER.   O question harsh and rude!
Love hath my death-blow given.

CHARON.   Never within my bark
May subject of that King o'erpass the
      River Dark.

THE LOVER.	Nay, Charon ; now of grace receive me for thy freight.
CHARON.	Another pilot seek ; for neither I nor Fate To touch his rights who rules the Gods may dare.
THE LOVER.	I go then spite of thee ; for in my soul I bear So many of Love's darts : such tears my fate deplore, That I myself will be both stream, and bark, and oar !

XXIV.

WIND'S LOVE.

SOFT Breeze, as to the leaves and flowers
    Thou bendest from above,
Thou dost not surely whisper low
    Vows of unchanging love?

Ah, ill for you, O scented flowers,
    And ill for you, bright leaves,
If any, hearkening to his sighs,
    Wind's word for truth receives!

Yes, fickle Wind, in spring and bloom
    Thy promises sound fair ;
Nor leaf nor bud would dream they all
    Are written in the air.

Dark Winter soon with icy hand
    Shall roughly bear away
The fragrance from the smiling flowers,
    The sunlight from the day.

The blight of death borne on thy wings
Shall nip each tender flower ;
And from each shivering tree be torn
The last leaf of its dower.

And thou, false Wind, shalt quite forget
That flowers' breath made thee sweet
When golden leaves and fair blooms lie
In mire beneath thy feet.

XXV.

HOME-SICKNESS.

(FROM A. SCHNEZLER).

When down our mountain side the snow-streams flow,
To the blue lake that heaven's face doth show,
The ox-bells tinkle forth their sweet refrain—
Shall I no more see Fatherland again?

When the Alphorn across the glacier rings,
From crag to crag the graceful chamois springs,
The eagle circling sweeps the azure plain—
Shall I no more see Fatherland again?

When smile green meads our Alpine vales among,
The village inn is gay with dance and song,
Each shepherd calls his love in well-known strain—
Shall I no more see Fatherland again?

When through the gorge the torrent madly falls,
From peak to peak the wrathful thunder calls,
The avalanche from far doth roar amain—
Shall I no more see Fatherland again?

When as night falls all round the mountains glow,
Day beckons, and the rose of dawn doth blow,
O heart, how still thou beatest in sore pain!—
Shall I no more see Fatherland again?

XXVI.

BABY'S FOOTMARKS.

I.

HUSHED a moment is the patter :
  At the open door she stands,
Fain to catch the " angels' feathers "
  In two dimpled baby hands.

Round the garden beds yet barren
  Now see little footprints lie,
When the first white snowdrop glimmers
  Fair beneath a grey March sky.

When the sunbeams kiss the daisies,
  Gaily dance the tiny feet,
As they chase the fleeting shadows—
  Was she, too, a shadow fleet ?

Through the quiet woodland pathways
  " So tired " baby footsteps steal ;
Fallen leaves beneath that rustle
  Such light pressure scarce could feel.

Ah ! a white cross gleameth newly
  Where their last faint trace appears :
O'er a tiny grass-mound softly
  Bending roses drop red tears !

II.

What did you see, O Baby,
   That turned your face away?
'Mid other opening blossoms
   Why could not you, too, stay?

Upon our earthly pathways
   Your treading was so brief,
Scarce could you spell the meaning
   Of human care or grief.

Dreamt you of happier meadows
   Where ne'er the roses weep,
Of skies across whose blueness
   Black storm-clouds never sweep?

Beyond our vision gazing
   With those blue wistful eyes,
For you, athwart our sunshine,
   Did sweeter light arise?

A pathway, Angel-guarded,
   Did you, perchance, behold,
From earth's rough deserts leading
   Straight to the sheltered Fold?

Ah, yes ; and in that Portal,
   Whose peace no foe alarms,
Methinks, a thorn-crowned Shepherd
   Who stood with out-stretched Arms!

XXVII.

THE DYING POET TO HIS WIFE.

(FROM THE ITALIAN OF G. REDAELLI).

O LIST the last faint speech of one
    For whom prepares the tomb!
As the last gift my hand may give,
    Take, Love, this withered bloom.

Thou knowest how my heart doth prize
    This flower that once was thine;
I stole it from thy breast-knot, Dear,
    The day that made thee mine.

A symbol then of love's sweet prime,
    But now of anguish sore,
Again upon thy bosom place
    This flower that blooms no more;

That, Love, within thy gentle heart
    Its form may graven be,
As once erewhile from thee 'twas borne,
    Once, given back to thee.

XXVIII.

STRAY BLOSSOMS.

(FROM RÜCKERT).

FRAIL bloom of Almond !
Ere Spring thou passest, flinging petals sweet,
A fragrant pathway for the March wind's feet.

Delicate Snowdrop !
The white veil lifts ; soft western breezes blow :
Thou stayest behind like a lost flake of snow.

Shy leaf-hid Violet !
"I go : the fair Rose cometh," thou dost say.
Full fair she comes ; yet, Sweet, do *thou* still stay.

Resplendent Lily !
In God's meet worship all the flowers hold part ;
Of that bright choir the white-stoled priest thou art.

Green Lily stem !
No nosegay's glories art thou made to share ;
But for God's Angel in his hand to bear.

XXIX.

SHUT DOORS.

(FROM RÜCKERT).

I HAVE knocked at the rich man's mansion fair :
A penny they flung from the window there.

I have knocked where red roses wreathe Love's door :
A crowd who sought entrance stood there before.

Where the Castle towers high I knocked full light :
" We open not here save to mounted knight."

I have sought where the house of peace might be :
There was none far and wide could show it me.

Yet I know one house more, a still and small ;
At its door shall my hand knock last of all.

Within it in truth is no lack of guest ;
Yet all in the low grave find room and rest.

XXX.

TO PSYCHE SLEEPING.

AH, wake not, Sweet One! nevermore
　　Shall thine be rest so deep;
Fair visions Love perchance may bring,
　　But never dreamless sleep.

The crimson roses steeped in sweet
　　Entwined around his bower
Hide thorns that leave a deeper stain—
　　Keep thou thy lotus flower!

O Psyche, love means woe, and tears
　　Wrung out in bitter pain,
Long vigils held in star-reft nights,
　　Grey mist, and falling rain.

No poppied sleep his eyes may seal
　　Whom Love's lips once have pressed;
A pilgrim clad in hempen robe
　　He wanders, seeking rest.

Sharp stones and briars wound hands and feet
　　Till, on the toilsome way,
From weary hands both staff and scrip
　　Death takes at close of day.

Yet Love hath wings that upward bear :
  The loss he brings is gain :
Therefore, O Soul, arise and win
  Long bliss by shortlived pain.

Each pang that seems a bitter death
  Shall fade, nor leave a smart ;
The crown of bliss such anguish gives
  Will nevermore depart.

Hold then the Wingéd Pilgrim's hand
  Till, raised beyond the stars,
His rest and thine shall both be won
  Where shine the crystal bars !

N

XXXI.

THE BLOSSOM OF PATIENCE.

(FROM RÜCKERT).

A BLOSSOM in the garden,
  I must in stillness wait
When, and in what sweet fashion,
  Thou bearest me my fate.

If thou a sunbeam comest,
  My petals shall unfold,
That all the joy thou beamest
  My heart may closely hold.

Be it as rain or dewdrop,
  Then, that it ne'er dry up,
I will shut fast the blessing
  In love's deep golden cup.

Or, if a soft wind passing,
  Thy presence be made known,
Then hear this low-bent blossom
  Murmur, " I am thine own."

A blossom in the garden,
  I must in stillness wait
When, and in what sweet fashion,
  Thou bearest me my fate.

XXXII.

ONE GUISE OF LOVE.

"There are many ways of loving."—A. A. PROCTOR.

THE love a silent harp might bear
    The wind that wakes its strings ;
Or leafless tree the heaven-sweet air
    Through which its verdure springs :

Such love as bears earth's panting breast
    To drops of cooling rain ;
Or the chased roe the covert blest
    That turns to peace her pain :

The love that draws in heaven's height
    Down to a mossy nest
The soaring lark, and turns his flight
    To that low place of rest :

Such love as Psyche sleeping feels
    When the long-waited kiss
The presence of a God reveals
    And wakens her to bliss :

The love that sees in all fair things
    The loved one's image shine ;
That gives the earth-born Angel wings—
    Such, if thou wilt, be thine.

January 5th, 1889.

XXXIII.

A DREAM OF DANTE.

I.

STAR-LOVING* Poet! as I read
    Thy melody sublime,
My trancéd soul with thee beheld
    Things not of earth or time.

Methought I entered by thy side
    The Land of endless Night,
The hopeless Realm that ne'er hath heard
    God's word, " Let there be light."

Black wings rushed by in stormy rack,
    The air was thick with sighs,
Blent with such tears as never fell
    On earth from human eyes.

Yet even in Hell we did not lose
    The sight of stars above,
Nor even there the music ceased
    First tuned by Primal Love.

---

* Each of the three divisions of Dante's *Divina Commedia* ends
with the word "stelle."

II.

From the eternal Prison-house
　　To breathe a clearer air
We came, where souls, though stained and sad,
　　Are lifted from despair

In that still Isle, where by God's grace,
　　Like fruit of holy pain,
Each reed the lapping wave doth wash,
　　When plucked, upsprings again.

Where from one fount two mystic streams
　　Flow down, a parted wave,
I stood, and in each healing flood
　　My soul, methought, did lave.

The steep ascent where souls grow pure
　　With labouring steps we trod,
And still above in their calm blue
　　Fair shone the stars of God.

III.

We came where heaven's " eternal pearl "
　　A lucent cloud appears ;
Then, borne by thirst that upward draws,
　　We soared among the spheres.

I marked, with heart that strove in vain
    To comprehend such bliss,
The Beatific Vision fill
    The eyes of Beatrice.

Bright wings swept by, a cloud of praise,
    As in that rapturous dream
From the clear Empyrean fell
    The snow-white rose's gleam.

Ah, then, no more a prisoned bird
    That beats its caging bars,
My heart grew still, for we had soared
    Beyond the realm of stars!

XXXIV.

SILVER AND GOLD.

STILL night hath come : the golden day
    Its radiant light forgetting,
Enwrapped in moonlight's tender veil
    Hath gained a silver setting.

The seasons roll.   Doth nature's hand
    Forget its lavish sweetness,
That she, for autumn's wealth of gold,
    Now gives the snow's white fleetness ?

Time turns his glass ; youth's clustering locks,
    A cloud of golden brightness,
Are changed beneath his frosty touch
    To crown of silver whiteness.

Hush !   Last of all, with gentle hand
    And presence unbeholden,
God's Angel stills life's silvern speech
    To silence that is golden.

XXXV.

THE ROSE.

THE Rose is dead.
Her leaves all shed.
Red drops that drain her heart
Now stain the grass
Where light feet pass
All heedless of her smart.

A long-drawn sigh
The breeze goes by
Whose voice was once a song :
She sits alone,
Who on her throne
Was Queen the flowers among.

Of all her dress
Of loveliness
Sharp thorns alone remain :
Of all her bliss
And sweet Love's kiss
A memory of pain.

XXXVI.

MY DOVE.

My Dove, on snow-white fleecy wing
  Why mountest thou so high,
Till like a "lonely cloud" thy form
  Shows pure against the sky?

Above the veiling mists of earth
  Thou soarest out of sight
To bathe thy snow-soft silver plumes
  In heaven's golden light.

Say, is it from thy wistful gaze
  Through windows of the skies,
That thou hast gained for love's delight
  The sweet look in thine eyes?

One day, when far beyond our ken
  Thou soaredst on swift wing,
Did Angels in soft whispers breathe
  The message thou dost bring?

O

Ah, Heaven-bound Bird, if heart's best love
  Hath power thy wing to hold,
One moment stay thy upward flight,
  Thy soaring pinions fold.

For, sweet Dove, may not those fleet wings
  That to the height have striven,
When love for their dear shadow sighs
  To brooding peace be given?

HUDSON AND SON, Printers, Edmund Street, Birmingham.

Opinions of the Press.

GRAPHIC.—"The book opens with a charming carol, 'A Christmas Legend,' translated from the German, where a little stranger child is depicted desolate in a stranger town. He prays as he rubs his little frost-chilled hand, and as answer we have the manifestation of the other Child, all of which is very prettily told. Among much that is nicely said, and will bear quoting, we may notice a sonnet, 'Paolo and Francesca,' suggested by the picture by Mr. G. F. Watts:

"In earth's sweet light erewhile they walked in pleasure,
   Seeing the fair sun rise, the pale stars shine
   Until the fatal hour that lit a flame unholy—
   Look in their faces and behold the sign ! "

QUEEN.—"Miss Postgate writes well and feelingly, and she will enlist the suffrages of not a few by publishing her little volume for the benefit of the work of S. Alban's, Birmingham."

TIME.—"Among these poems are many that would find a fitting place in our hymnals. The poem in memory of the late Rev. A. H. Mackonochie is a particularly striking and graceful piece of writing. The translations from the French, German, and Italian, represent very happily the spirit of the originals. The author's version of Sully Prudhomme's exquisite but untranslatable lyric, 'O vous qui m'aiderez dans mon agonie,' is worthy of note."

LITERARY WORLD.—"The religious verses in Miss Postgate's 'Christmas Legend' show much devout and tender feeling."

GOSPELLER.—"The writer ·has plainly written because 'the numbers came.' Where old thoughts that belong to all are used, they are freshly put forth from a mind that has made them its own, and realised their meaning from itself. There is no expression of feeling in any line which does not bear on it plain marks of having been felt. Even the translations are not like many, the work of a rhymer who has a dictionary. They shew a sympathy of spirit between the original author and the interpreter. The book is valuable for the beauty of its sentiment and the music of its words. It seems to be even more so, for its truth and earnestness, and high and pure aim."

CENTRAL LITERARY MAGAZINE.—"This charming little volume.
. . . We would call special attention to the 'Good Physician' in the former part and to 'The Dead Lark' in the latter. All the poems are characterised by a religious tone of thought and refinement of expression."

BIRMINGHAM AND MIDLAND INSTITUTE MAGAZINE.—The book includes several charming poems suggested by some of the masterpieces of literature, five being on Shaksperian subjects. . . . We very earnestly commend this little volume to all who take an interest in our local literature, and, indeed, to all who love true poetry. In harmony of metre, in grace of expression, and in refinement of feeling, these poems will take their place by the best of the kind our town has produced."

BIRMINGHAM DAILY POST.—"The 'Carmina Sacra' are musical and refined. . . . In the second part there are several very graceful poems, and one group, dealing with Shakspere's heroines, is very successful, tender, sympathetic, and penetrative. The dainty little poem, 'Iris,' is a fair example of the quality of the verse."

BIRMINGHAM DAILY GAZETTE.—"The poems are simple in style, and convey with force and directness high and good truths. Many of those in the first part of the volume are genuine hymns. . . . They are impressed with deep religious sentiment. The second part of the volume consists of miscellaneous verses, which are of a pleasing nature. Miss Postgate devotes some of them to subjects and characters that the great English poets have made immortal. Thus we get lines on 'Cordelia,' 'Desdemona,' 'Ophelia,' and 'Evelyn Hope'—the last-named poem, under the title of 'The Waking,' being a message to him who had mourned 'beautiful Evelyn Hope is dead.'

> "She lay at sunset sleeping,
> Your leaf in her sweet cold hands ;
> With dawn her soul hath wakened ;
> She remembers and understands.

Some of these poems have a fervour and passion for which the previous part of the volume had not prepared us, and in the translations from the French, German, and Italian, Miss Postgate not only shows proficiency in transplanting flowers of poesy from their native to English soil, but also succeeds in making them retain their rich colouring. 'Circe' is a poem that exhibits the influence of the Rossetti school ; but the poems as a whole, are singularly free from imitations, and clearly testify that Miss Postgate has a natural vein of poetry."

WAKEFIELD FREE PRESS.—"A charming volume. . . . The poems are full of graceful thoughts happily expressed. The book is a pleasing and welcome contribution to the poetry of the period, and it will doubtless obtain a hearty welcome from lovers of true poetry."